SWEET DISTRACTION

Lainey Davis

Sweet Distraction
Stag Brothers Book One
By Lainey Davis

© 2018 Lainey Davis

Join my mailing list and never miss a new release!
laineydavis.com

Many thanks to Nicky Lewis for editorial input.

Thank you for supporting
independent authors!

CHAPTER ONE
Tim

I'm not sure why I keep trying to get things accomplished in the office. When I'm here, I'm interrupted constantly. Everyone has questions and apparently I'm the only one with any answers. I'm trying to review the notes from our top clients, but my email chimes every few seconds and I've already had to put my cell on silent because my family evidently needs me to manage them, too.

When my intercom buzzes, I'm in the middle of re-reading a sentence I've started about ten times, so I'm impatient with my admin. "What, Donna? What??"

"I apologize, Mr. Stag. It can wait."

I exhale. Inhale again, exhale. What did that corporate meditation expert tell me I should do? Three long deep breaths before speaking? Who has time?? "No, I'm the one who should apologize for my tone, Donna. What's up?"

"It's just that Ms. Peterson is here to meet with you."

"Peterson?" A glance at my calendar shows only "busy" for the next half hour. It's not like Donna to be vague when scheduling. Who the hell is Ms. Peterson?

I hate feeling caught off guard. This never happens, and I don't tolerate it. But I have no idea what Donna is talking about, and that makes me nervous. I'm always prepared for meetings. That's what I do. I prepare for things, explore every possible avenue, make a plan for each contingency. That's how I steered my family through crisis and how I managed to run my own multi-million dollar company before I hit 30.

"Remember, Mr. Stag?" Donna's voice is calm. "Your grandmother suggested we bring on a chef and when I asked at the culinary school, they said--"

"Oh! The chef! Ms. Peterson is the chef. Right." As usual, my grandmother has been inserting herself into my affairs and, as usual, she's probably right. But I can't have her interfering with my work. I make a mental note to speak with my grandmother about making arrangements with Donna without my consent. "Donna, can you take her for some coffee or something while I prepare for our discussion?"

"She says that she's already had coffee today and that--"

"Give me five minutes, Donna. Then send her in."

"Yes, sir."

What kinds of questions should I even be asking a chef? I should have just left this interview up to Donna. My grandmother took one look at me last weekend and decided I'm pale because I don't eat properly. She's not wrong--I work 18-hour days and usually don't remember to eat until every place is closed. When I get here in the morning, nothing is open yet. I know my staff works hard for me, too, and I actually really like my grandmother's idea to have a chef come in so they can feel appreciated at lunch and maybe eat something good in the afternoon. I click through my research. A lot of big companies are bringing in a chef, having lunch together as a team every day. My competitors aren't--it's mostly tech companies. But the research seems sound. A small investment toward food and the chef's salary for greater retention and improved morale. Who says you can't buy loyalty with pie?

When Donna knocks at my office door, I look up from my monitor and, for the second time today, I'm caught totally off guard.

Standing beside my secretary is the most striking woman I've ever seen in my life. In an office full of power suits and smooth hair, Ms. Peterson stands out like a star in the night sky. Her blonde curls are unruly, messily held back with what looks like a pen. Maybe it's a chopstick? She can't be more than 5'2", even in black clogs, which she wears with chef whites and a hot pink scarf. The shapeless jacket pulls taut across what I can tell is a full bust, and suddenly all I can think about is peeling her out of that double-breasted coat so I can massage the creamy, white globes it hides.

"And this is Mr. Stag, of course, head of the company. Mr. Stag, this is Alice Peterson." She sticks out a hand and I meet her eyes, pleasantly surprised by her firm grasp as she pumps my hand.

"It's a pleasure to be here, Mr. Stag," she says, and smiles. She has one of those smiles that reaches her entire face, and I'm mesmerized by her violet eyes as Donna excuses herself and backs from the room. The click of the closing door shakes me back to the present and I gesture for her to take a seat.

Suddenly my mahogany desk is too big and too wide; the space between us seems too far. *This isn't going to work at all,* I decide. I can't have someone like this distracting me at work. I sigh, thinking of how I'll explain to Donna that she has to find someone less…tempting. I realize as I'm thinking these thoughts that I absolutely cannot *not* hire her because she turns me on. I should know. I'm a lawyer and we specialize in injury and wrongful termination cases.

I realize the silence has become uncomfortably long when she asks me, hesitantly, "So…what would you like to ask me?"

I meet those violet eyes again and tell myself to go into work mode. This is just another puzzle for me to solve. How to overcome the lust I'm feeling for this woman. Just another obstacle. "Well, I've never hired a chef before, to be honest, but it's something a lot of companies are doing these days."

She nods. "Oh for sure. It's definitely something companies are using to differentiate themselves and attract top talent. Everyone seems to have a 'thing,' you know? Fancy milkshakes or an all-day cereal buffet…"

When I don't say anything, she continues, rambling a bit. "I took a look around your lunch room before I signed in with your admin. You don't have a ton of space down there, but I was definitely thinking we can work on power bowls. Protein packed, quick meals. Nothing heavy on the garlic."

My wit fails me and I can't think of a response, so I say nothing. *She must think I'm an idiot or an asshole,* I tell myself as I sit there, speechless. I sigh. "It sounds like you have the right idea. Hiring a chef was actually suggested to me by someone who noticed we work long hours. My attorneys are very dedicated and by the time they remember they haven't refueled, most delivery places are closed. None of us wants to rely on fast food."

She nods. "Quick, nutritious meals, ready to eat. You guys need protein and fat if you're cranking out hours like that. Lots of fresh fruit. Nothing that will stain your dress shirt." And then she winks, causing me to glance at my chest. I'm relieved to discover there is no stain.

I clear my throat. "So Donna tells me you did very well in culinary school?"

Alice Peterson perks right up at this. I can tell she's proud of her accomplishments. "I finished top of my class," she says. "My family worked *really* hard to get me there, so I wanted to honor that by doing my best. I've always wanted to be a chef!" She beams. "I even got to intern with Kevin Souza before he closed Salt of the Earth," she says, referencing what had been my favorite restaurant to take clients before the chef/owner closed it to focus on a new concept a few towns over.

"Well," I say, impressed, "Why don't you tell me what I should be asking you."

She nods and stands. "I think we should go look at the space and talk about what's missing."

"Oh," I say, rising. "I hadn't considered that you might need different equipment." My firm occupies the top two floors of one of the skyscrapers in downtown Pittsburgh. When we leased the space five years ago, I knew the former occupants had also been a law firm. As we walk toward the break room, I realize that of course she would need ovens and stoves and an industrial refrigerator if she's going to prepare multiple meals for us every day.

Alice begins talking about her favorite appliance vendor and I lose myself in her speech, which seems to come so easily to her.

Her words aren't measured or calculated. When she tells me that Don's is the best appliance dealer for a Viking range, I can tell she really feels this way, and not because she has a reciprocal deal with him.

"What would your ideal meal look like here at work, Mr. Stag," she asks, frowning and pulling out a notebook from the pocket of that bulky coat.

I squint, looking around the small break room. Right now, it's got a standard fridge and sink and electric range. It resembles the kitchen of a college dorm…with a few circular tables scattered around. "I really liked what I read about one of the tech companies in East Liberty," I say. "They have a large space where they all eat lunch together every day, even the CEO. The chef rings a dinner bell when it's time to eat." I remember reading that and thinking of family dinners at my childhood home, before everything turned sour.

My mother used to ring an old ship's bell to summon my brothers and me in from the back yard as soon as she saw my father's car approaching our driveway. Lost in the memory, I'm jolted again when Alice touches my arm.

CHAPTER TWO

Alice

I finally couldn't resist touching him, not another second. I just had to feel what would happen. Even through the layers of his suit coat and shirt, I can feel a surge of electricity when my fingers make contact with the rock-hard arm of Tim Stag.

If I didn't need this job so badly, I'd say screw it and shove him against the wall right here in the break room. His grey eyes seem to shift with his mood, looking out from a sweep of short, chestnut hair. Right now, I want to brush that hair back from his skin and shove my tongue down his throat. But, duty calls, and so I pull myself together and decide I'm going to land this job with this brooding, handsome man as my boss.

"Mr. Stag," I say, and his wide eyes meet mine, impossible to read. I pull back my hand and gesture around me. "You're going to have to knock down a wall and put in a serving line." He nods, but doesn't say anything, so I continue. "We can put glass-front coolers over here where I can keep grab-n-go meals and snacks ready. A long row of tables down the middle should be nice. With the wall gone, you'll get natural light and a view of the Point," I say, nodding toward where the city's three rivers converge outside our office.

"We can even do some booths along that wall, if you ever wanted to have clients here for lunch. Or just want more private conversation space."

"And are you able to oversee that renovation? Manage everything you need to get started?" His voice is so deep. I long to put my hand against his chest and feel it reverberate.

My eyes go wide at his question, though. I mean, yeah. I can figure all that stuff out. My dad works construction and my brother sells industrial kitchen appliances. I just can't believe I might *get* to do something like that. I was sure my first cooking gig would be frying burgers at one of the sports stadiums. When my favorite instructor told me her best friend's boss was looking for a corporate chef, I read absolutely everything I could find about this place.

Tim Stag is a hotshot lawyer. Stone cold. He's never lost a case and managed to land the players associations for the professional hockey, football, *and* baseball teams here in Pittsburgh. He finished college *and* law school early, nailed the bar exam, and thinks he needs a corporate chef to help his company stand out. Maybe he doesn't know how much he stands out? His photos online did him no justice. The man is a fox. I realize he's still waiting for me to answer. "I mean, do you have the budget for that sort of project?"

He waves his hand as if that's irrelevant. *Must be nice*, I think. He leans past me to grab a bottle of water from the counter and I smell him--some sort of sporty deodorant mixed with the clean smell of nice soap and...something uniquely male. There's a power scent that's 100% Tim Stag. I watch his Adam's apple move as he swallows a sip of the water. "What I don't have, Ms. Peterson, is time. You can work with Donna to start the renovation. The job is yours if you want it."

"Really? You didn't even really ask me anything. Don't you want to know, I don't know, what my philosophy is? Or if I'm a vegan or something?"

He raises one dark eyebrow at me, his eyes questioning. "Are you a vegan?"

I laugh. "You think I'd be shaped like this if I never ate cheese?" I immediately regret drawing his attention to my body, which is thankfully masked in my chef whites. I flush. "No," I quickly correct myself. "I'm definitely an omnivore." I hold my hand out for a shake, saying, "I'd love to join Stag Law. When can I start?"

I brace myself for the jolt I know is coming when he returns my handshake. I feel the sizzle right through to my core when our skin makes contact, just like I felt when I first walked into his office. I hold his dark gaze and smile, imagining what it will be like to see him every day, lost in a fantasy where I feed him something delectable and he groans with pleasure.

He frowns, looking around. "Can you start right away? I guess you can't do anything with what's here now?"

I can't help but laugh, because I cook meals for my family most days in a space half this size. "What time do you want me to serve lunch?"

He walks me down the hall and leaves me with Donna, who sets me up with a corporate credit card. Two hours later, I'm plating tiny sandwiches with fruit skewers, dishes of hummus with sliced veggies and pita wedges. I've got several carafes of cucumber water scattered around the room just as the first curious employees start poking in their heads. "Help yourself," I tell them.

Soon I'm chatting with everyone, asking them for their favorite snacks and taking notes about their eating habits, things to consider about their work day. I hit it off with a woman named Juniper, who says she's new here, too. "I'm not quite sure what to make of the boss man," I confide in Juniper, smiling as she takes a hearty portion of the various sandwiches.

She nods. "I know. He's sort of hard to read. I was offered this position after a phone interview, so I wasn't sure what to expect, but he is assigning me to represent his brother, so he must trust me!"

I see Donna enter the room and I pat Juniper's arm, which is surprisingly firm. "Hey I gotta go talk to Donna, but I'll talk to you later, ok? Nice biceps by the way."

Juniper laughs. "I row crew," she tells me. "You should check it out sometime. You could be our coxswain."

Vowing to google that later, I head off with Donna to make a plan for the renovation, as well my ideas to feed everyone while that's taking place. I tell Donna that I think we should order biodegradable plates and cutlery until we can get a dishwasher set up. She just nods and tells me to do whatever I think is best.

How amazing is that? Three hours ago I was just a jobless graduate from the shabby part of Highland Park. Now, I have my very own office. I can hardly believe my luck. I'm 24 years old and the week I finish culinary school, I land my first full-time job with total autonomy and an unlimited budget. I definitely owe my instructor a flower delivery for recommending me!

My first order of business is to call up my dad--who else would I hire for a construction project? I decide to use the office phone to see if I can surprise my father. When he answers with a chipper, "This is Bob. How can I help you?" I respond with, "Yes, this is Stag Law calling. We're looking for Robert Peterson."

There's a pause on the line and Dad says, "Alice? Sweetie is that you?"

I share the great news with my dad. I know I'm talking fast, but I can't help it. I tell him that I got the job (at the top of the salary range for corporate chefs, too) and free reign over the renovation to get their kitchen up to snuff. "We are going to hire you to do the project for us, Dad! Can you come take a look?"

"Well, Pumpkin, that is fantastic," he says. "You know, we just finished a renovation in that building, too. Some insurance company redid their layout. Why don't I bump my first estimate tomorrow and drive you in to work and take a gander at it?"

Dad asks some basic questions about the project and jokes that I should just make everyone garlic wings with extra ranch to drip all over their designer suits. "Very funny, Dad. But I can make those for you tonight if you want. We could celebrate, get some growlers from Grist House."

"Anything you want, Pumpkin. You know, your mother would be so proud of you." His voice cracks a little and I can tell he's tearing up. My mom passed away from breast cancer 8 years ago. Things have been rough for us since then. Medical bills almost crushed us and we lost Mom anyway. I don't know how my dad managed to scrape together tuition for me to go to culinary school. I kept my job waiting tables and went part-time for years until I finally finished.

I think about my mom's words during our last conversation.

She told me to go after my dreams, even if it felt difficult. "I know she'd be proud, Dad, but thanks. I want to get things set up here for tomorrow, but I should be home around 5:30 I think." We hang up, and I get to work stocking the Stag Law break room with snacks and muffins for the morning. I've started stacking all my new equipment in my office, both because there's nowhere else to put it and because I still can't believe it's all mine. I was dancing through the aisles at Restaurant Depot outfitting the basic kitchen, placing my order for spices and bulk produce. Soon, I'll go meet with one of the local farms and set up an account for herbs and eggs. Oh, and dairy.

I'm so lost in my plans I don't notice Tim Stag watching me. When I look up, realizing I've been singing out loud, his intense expression   freezes   me   in   my   tracks.

CHAPTER THREE
Tim

Sorry if I frightened you," I say, realizing she looks alarmed. "I shouldn't have stood here staring. I just…everything smells so good."

Her face lights up behind the mountain of mixing bowls. "These muffins are for tomorrow morning," she says. "I'm just about to slide in the last batch."

Since I saw her last, she's tamed her curls back into a tight braid and tied the pink scarf around her head. Despite having made a lunch my associates won't stop talking about and what looks to be several hundred muffins, she still looks pristine in her white coat. And too fucking modest. Her pink tongue slips out as she hoists a pan into the oven, and I long to taste it, to lose my fingers in that nest of blond curls. Shaking my head, I realize that coat might not be modest enough. I have to pull myself together and remember that this woman is now my employee. She distracts me, and I don't like that.

I might need to go out and find someone looking for a quick release. How long has it been since I've been with a woman? I try to run the calculations, but Alice walks around the table with a muffin. "Here," she says, her face eager. "Taste!"

I raise an eyebrow, but accept the muffin from her and venture a bite. What hits my mouth is the most delicious flavor combination I think I've ever experienced. The muffin is moist and citrusy, but somehow light and hearty all at once. And there's an aftertaste I can't put my finger on. Alice must see me struggling to identify the flavor, because she begins talking in that carefree, delighted voice.

"They're lemon lavender," she tells me, "but I added flax for protein and used sour cream for texture. I also did a banana muffin with whole wheat and...oh. Am I rambling? I tend to get excited. I've been tweaking these recipes for awhile now. I am going to do some smoothies for the morning, too!"

A timer begins to beep and she bends to pull another tray of muffins from the oven. I stare, open-mouthed, at her perfect ass. It's round and tight, and I'm pretty sure each cheek would fill one of my hands. I swallow the rest of the muffin, trying not to think about slapping her backside as I pound into her from behind, right here in the break room. "Alice, they're delicious," I manage to say.

She moves quickly and expertly, wrapping the food in plastic and making piles to wash up at the sink. "I'm already glad we brought you on board. Donna got you everything you need, I presume?"

She laughs then, a hearty sound that explodes out of her. "*Presume*," she says in a mock-low voice, then claps her hand over her mouth. I feel the side of my face pull up in a grin. *She's making fun of me. How long has it been since anyone other than my brothers has made fun of me?* "Fuck," she says. "I'm so sorry. Shit, now I said fuck at work."

"Welcome aboard," I say, laughing quietly. "I always appreciate it when someone calls me out on my bullshit." She still looks horrified, so I try to reassure her I'm not upset. "I've spent my whole career in litigation or talking with judges. I guess I do sound a little pompous sometimes. It's hard to turn that off."

Alice is easy to talk to, and I make note of that. She's someone who might cause me to let my guard down, and if there's one thing I've learned, it's that I can never, ever stop being vigilant. "Well anyway," she says, "Donna's been great and I have a contractor coming tomorrow to give an estimate on the renovation. I hope you don't mind that I called my father's company for that. He's very well known for commercial construction throughout Pittsburgh."

"I don't see why that would be a problem," I say. "You've already impressed me with what you accomplished in one day, and I *presume* he taught you your work ethic. I trust your judgment." My personal cell begins to ring and a glance tells me it's my brother calling. "Excuse me," I say to Alice. "I have to take this. Thank you for your efforts today." I hurry into the hall to take the call as I walk back to my office. "Ty. What's up?"

"What, did I interrupt you with a woman, asshole? You sound so flustered."

"Nice to hear from you, too, little brother."

He busts my balls for awhile before he reminds me that tonight is his welcome home dinner. My kid brother is a professional hockey player. He's been playing in Vancouver for the past few years, and then got sent to marinate in the minors. He was traded to the Pittsburgh Fury this year. Of course he hired my firm to handle his contract. It took some finesse to get him called back up from the minor leagues in time for playoffs, because my brother has a bit of a temper on the ice. We're all thrilled to have him back home where he belongs.

I'm the oldest of 3 brothers, and we're all about 18 months apart, so we've always been tight. When our mom died, we had to stick together. Our father never recovered from the shock of losing her, so it's really been the 3 of us Stag brothers. Having Ty so far away for 3 years has made everything feel off-kilter.

"Listen, dick wad, Gran says I'm supposed to tell you to be on time. I'm a client AND family, so that makes me double important now. She's got drinks starting at 6:30."

"Yeah, yeah, I got it." I look at my watch. "I've got to finish up some paperwork and I'll head over. You still staying with her until you find a place?"

"Fuck yeah I'm staying with Gran. She treats me like a god. Plus then I'm not tempted to bring home any puck bunnies." Ty proceeds to describe his most recent evening with some fan he met in a club, and I have to tune him out before his play-by-play leads me toward inappropriate thoughts about Alice.

I hang up with my brother and open my laptop. I love it here at the office when nobody else is around. No distractions. Just me and my files. I start reading through the case briefing for one of our athletes who is entering contract negotiations, but even with nobody here to call me with questions, I still can't concentrate. My mind keeps slipping back to Alice Peterson and her violet eyes. And her perfect ass in those awful pants.

After 20 minutes or so, I realize it's a lost cause trying to get anything done today. The thought of Alice stirring that muffin batter keeps taking over my thoughts. I decide that maybe if I rub one out, it'll clear my head, and so I lock my office door and sit on my leather couch.

I close my eyes and it takes less than a second before I'm rock hard, imagining her full lips and that sweet tongue latching on to my cock as if it's one of her delicious confections. I begin to stroke my rod, picturing her firm grip on my base as those blond curls bob up and down. Faster than I would have thought, I feel my balls tighten and I cum, spraying forcefully onto my chest. A groan escapes my lips and I feel myself spurt again and again until I'm breathless.

"Fuck," I mutter, seeing that I've spoiled my tie. I didn't even have time to grab the tissues. I'm like a teenage boy ripping open my pants to beat off at work. What the hell has happened to my self control? I rip the tie from my neck and open my bottom drawer where I keep my backup wardrobe. I never risk having to appear before a judge, or even a client for that matter, looking less than my best.

Using the mirror in the corner of my office, I slip on the clean tie and straighten my hair. I text my car service and exhale, walking toward the elevator. As I pass the break room, I see Alice has set everything up for breakfast tomorrow, and I smile. She's good at what she does. The entire car ride to my grandmother's house, I'm distracted by thoughts of my new corporate chef, her curls, and her curves.

I decide to ask my brother Thatcher to introduce me to someone. I'm too wound up lately. He knows tons of artsy women. I'm sure he can find me someone discrete, looking for what I am seeking, too: dinner and a fast fuck, back to the office by 6am. *Yes*, I nod. *That's exactly what I need.*

CHAPTER FOUR

Alice

I parallel park my tiny Honda Civic in the space in front of our house, leaving the driveway for my sister Amy's minivan. These days, it's pretty unusual for adult children to stay living with their parents like this, but the Peterson family loves being together. The four of us kids have stuck together even more since Mom died.

My Dad still owns the giant house where we grew up. He converted the third floor into an apartment when my sister got married and told them to stay until they got their feet under them. They've got a separate entrance and everything. She and her husband have pretty good jobs--she's a nurse and he's a teacher like our mother was--but it's hard to let go of having family so close.

I spend a *lot* of time watching her kids while she's at work. Between me and my brother Dan, my sister never has to use daycare. I guess that's going to change now that I've landed myself such a cool job. I pull my arms to my chest and hug myself, reminding myself that this *is* all real and not some fantasy I dreamed up.

I grab the bags of groceries from the back and pick up the growlers of beer. I practically dance inside and shout to Dan that I'm home and I'm making wings.

"Sweet! That must mean you got the gig, hey sis?" Dan is a year older than me, but he still lives with Dad, too. He sells commercial appliances, and he really knows his stuff. As I cook,

I fill him in on the renovation and assure him I'll be placing an order as soon as Dad gets the bid sent over. Between our dad working in construction, my brother Ryan working as a mechanic, and my sister working as a nurse, there isn't much we need to look for outside our immediate family. Dad's brother's an electrician, and one of his sons is a plumber, so we've got our bases covered. My family all looks out for each other, and I wouldn't have it any other way.

Amy comes floating in the door with my nephews. She pecks my cheek as she pours a glass of beer. She takes a sip and her eyes go wide. "This is really good, Al. What is this?"

"Undead Unicorn," I tell her. "It'll go great with the wings if you can wait ten minutes and not drink it all." I flick her with a dishtowel I've got slung over my shoulder and tell my siblings about my new job. "I have complete independence over all of it," I gush. "Whatever I want to cook. I'm my own boss. Sort of. I mean I guess Mr. Stag is my boss-boss, but he told me to do what I think is best."

"Mr. Stag?" My brother teases me, but my sister raises an eyebrow.

"Which Stag?" she asks. "We went to high school with them."

I shake my head. "I never went to school with anyone named Stag. I'd remember them, trust me. But my boss is Tim."

She sighs. "Ah, Tim Stag. Do you know his full name is Timber?"

She runs for the bookshelves in the living room where my dad has kept every book we've ever owned. She slides out her old yearbook. Amy is the oldest, so I guess that would put her around my boss's age. "Here," she says, sliding the book across the counter.

There he is glaring up from the page, looking as intense then as he did today. Dark hair, unreadable grey eyes. Chiseled jaw line. "That's him," I say.

"Timber Stag," my brother chimes in. "Who names their kid Timber?"

Amy flips the pages and we find Thatcher Stag in my brother Ryan's year. "I swear there was another one," she says. "Maybe he went to a magnet school or something? Anyway, spill it, Al. Does he still look this good?"

I nod and tell her about wanting to jump his bones in the kitchen. "Gross, Alice. Come on!" my brother feigns disgust and leaves the room with his beer, but Amy leans across the counter while I finish making dinner.

"And Aim, he smells ah-maze-ing. Not that I spent all day sniffing him, but I caught a whiff. And it was nice."

She nods, looking dreamily at the picture. "He was always sort of standoffish in school. Super serious. I remember him just always being…intense."

"He'd have to be, to build such a successful law practice at his age. Everyone at the office is super driven." I start to tell her about meeting the staff at lunch. "Oh! The third brother is Ty. He plays hockey. My new friend Juniper is going to be his attorney. She was telling me how she was excited that Tim assigned her to be his brother's new lawyer."

My sister laughs when I tell her Juniper suggested I try crew. She pulls out her phone and looks up the rowing team here in Pittsburgh. "Look how fit everyone is," Amy says. "Maybe you should sign up to make them lunch after their workout."

"Very funny, Aim. I'll have you know I keep in shape chasing your sons around." I pause then, remembering that I'm not going to be able to watch them during the day anymore. "Speaking of, we're going to have to talk about my schedule." I start to carry the platters of food to the table as the back door opens and my dad walks in to the kitchen.

"There's my pumpkin patch," says Dad as my nephews swarm around his legs. He plants a kiss on each of us. Amy texts her husband, Doug, to come down for dinner. The seven of us dig in and I smile, thinking how fortunate I am.

Dad and I talk about the renovation and how something like that should only take a few weeks if he lights the right fire under his crew. "Which I will, Pumpkin, don't you worry about that." He tells me that as soon as he can get permits in place, he can get started. "If budget really is no issue, that is," he winks.

My brother and my nephews begin bickering about the newest

Ninjago movie and I just feel so content looking around at my family. Our lives are so different now than they might have been if my mother hadn't gotten sick. But even as she was dying, she always told us we needed to stick together, to help each other.

I'm reminded again how I'm leaving my sister high and dry for childcare. I hadn't been expecting the job to begin right away, and I know it's not so easy to just find two daycare spaces with no notice. "Hey Aim," I say, whispering across the table. "What will you do with Ethan and Eli? Mr. Stag was pretty serious about me starting right away."

She furrows her brow. "Well, I don't work again until Friday. That gives me a few days to make calls. Honestly, Al, I don't want you to worry about it. I knew you'd be job hunting when you finished school. I really should have had a plan in place by now." Her husband, Doug, starts helping us brainstorm stopgap childcare options until they can find a place for the boys. They wonder aloud if he should cancel his commitment to teach summer school, but Amy shakes her head.

"Really, it's only for a few more months," she says. "Ethan starts kindergarten in the fall. God, I can't believe he's going to school already."

As they all start to reminisce about my precocious older nephew, my mind slips back to my new job and all the recipes I want to put in place. If I really work hard this week, I'm pretty sure I can get to where I'll be mostly in my office on Friday except for serving and cleaning up lunch. "Hey, Aim, I bet I can bring the boys with me on Friday," I tell her. "I'll just be doing admin stuff by then and they can play in my office when I'm serving lunch."

She looks at me with a severe sort of scowl.

"What?" I say. "They were desperate to have me there. I'll just let someone know I might have the boys this one time."

She frowns, and says, "I somehow can't see Tim Stag feeling excited about a pair of rambunctious boys running around his law firm, Alice. How about we save that for a last resort."

Nodding, I start to clean up, thoughts of meals for the staff racing through my mind.

CHAPTER FIVE

Tim

The rest of the week proves just as distracting as Monday, and it sets me into a foul mood. I'd subjected myself to my brothers' merciless taunting when I asked Thatcher to set me up with someone this week, and after all of that, he still hasn't found anyone. I'm starting to think I'm going to rub my dick raw trying to find release every morning in the shower, since I'm waking up hard as steel after dreaming about *her* each night.

I've never met a woman who leaves me so beside myself. I'm not sure what it is about her, especially since I've been deliberate about keeping my distance. She's wild and fearless, joyful and light. I've always craved order and predictability. I operate from a place of reason. I interpret the law very rigidly, and I bring my clients a lot of satisfaction. When I date, it's always for a very specific reason. And I don't bother very often.

I maintain my family's finances, manage their real estate deals, even track their preventative healthcare for them so nothing is in disarray. That is how I keep everyone safe. Except my father, but I learned long ago that you can't help someone determined to destroy himself.

Rifling through a folder on my desk, I can't seem to find what I'm looking for and I buzz Donna. I shout her name and realize, again, I need to get a grip on my tone. "What can I do for you, Mr. Stag?"

I take a deep breath. "Donna, I can't find the briefing on the Jergensmater case."

"All the briefs for this week's priority cases are in the red folder on your desk, Mr. Stag. I compiled everything that needed your immediate attention."

Of course she's right. Everything I need for this case is right in front of me, along with the notes for our other contract negotiations, an injury dispute, and leads on new business that some of my top associates have brought in. "Donna, I'm not sure what I'd do without you," I tell her.

"That's what I'm here for, sir! Would you like me to schedule you for a massage next week? You seem a little worked up." I thank her and tell her to go for it as I make a mental note to give her a raise.

I scan the files I need, but I feel restless. I look at the clock and realize I haven't eaten anything today. Shit. It's eleven. If I go to the break room now, Alice Peterson will be prepping for the lunch rush and I'll have to avoid inhaling her scent as I walk close to her to take some of the food that's destined to be the best thing I've ever eaten.

I weigh the effects of asking Donna to grab me something and feel guilty at the thought of interrupting her work because I'm worried I can't control my dick near the new chef. I pull out my phone and text my brother. *No leads for me for tonight I guess?*

Sorry, T-dog. Can't find anyone desperate enough. You know, Timber, there's this thing called Tinder…

Yeah, yeah. Thanks for nothing.

Little Bro says you've got a new lady lawyer on your staff. Maybe I should test drive her for you?

Stay the fuck away from my employees, Thatcher. That goes double for Ty.

I start to walk to the kitchen, even more pissed off that I can't find a fucking date for myself. Then I start to wonder why this suddenly bothers me so much, since I have never really sought a woman for…I don't know if I'm looking for comfort or if I just want to get laid. The whole situation has me unnerved. I keep walking, and I hear something very unsettling.

Why the hell are there children in my office? Lying on the floor over some sort of tablet device, a pair of tow-headed boys laughs at some animated show with burping slugs.

"What is the meaning of this?" My voice is loud and stern. The kids gasp and look up at me like they might cry. I've put on my courtroom voice before thinking twice. "This is absolutely unacceptable. Who brought these children here?"

Alice Peterson's head appears behind a stack of food trays. "Oh, gosh, Mr. Stag, you scared me. Are they in your way?"

"What they are is in my *office*," I reply. I can feel a vein starting to bulge in my neck. "What if a client were to come in here? And they're lying on the *floor*. This is utterly inappropriate. Are these your children?" Before I can stop myself, I'm laying into her about her inconsiderate choice to burden us in our professional workplace. By the time I finish, my hands are clenched into fists and Alice Peterson looks like she's going to either cry or murder me.

Juniper Jones, my new associate, steps into the break room, frowning. "What's the commotion?"

I hold up a hand to her. "This doesn't concern you, Ms. Jones. I was discussing Miss Peterson's decision to bring children into our place of business without consulting me."

"Excuse me, but I talked to Donna about it--"

"Donna? Is Donna your boss? Does Donna sign your paychecks?"

Juniper steps in between Alice and me, as the kids run behind the counter toward Alice. "Woah. Tim. Enough. You're out of line here with your tone." She's right, of course. My chest is heaving, I'm so worked up over this, and the worst part is that I can't quite put a finger on why this is so upsetting for me.

Juniper walks toward Alice and draws her in for a hug. "You ok, Al?" I see Alice nod and hear them murmuring together. I hear Alice mutter the word "asshole" and I know she's right.

I take a few deep breaths and say, "I apologize that my tone got heated. Miss Peterson, may I see you in my office after you serve lunch?"

She nods, and I add, "Please see that the children find somewhere else to spend the afternoon." I stride toward the new, glass-front coolers and grab two random containers from inside and storm back to my office.

I pull up the folder of notes on Alice Peterson. I read her resume and quickly determine that she's about 24 years old. As I gulp down an amazing--*of course it's amazing, Alice made it--*fruit smoothie with some sort of zesty aftertaste, I realize what enrages me about this situation. *Alice has a family,* I think. Some man has been inside her and she has carried his children. She belongs to someone else, and that means she can't ever be mine.

This won't do at all. I do not respond very well to limits. I buzz Donna and ask her to come into my office.

She glides into the space she helped me design. The corner office with two sides of vast windows, lush carpet. I might be the fire and the brain behind this organization, but Donna is the thread that ties it together. "Hey, Donna," I ask. "Did you give Miss Peterson permission to bring children into the office today?"

She nods. "I did. Alice asked me about it on Wednesday, told me she had been working all week to get the renovation to a stopping place and map out all the menus and ordering. She seemed to have a handle on things, and I said I didn't see the harm if they stayed in her office, especially since we hired her on such short notice. Did something happen?"

I exhale and put my hands behind my head, staring out my window at the confluence of the rivers below. I can see families walking around in the park on this warm summer day, and I wonder whether Alice has called the children's father--*her man,* I think, bitterly--to come fetch the boys. "No, nothing like that. I just came upon them and wasn't expecting to see them. I might have lost my temper. You know I don't like surprises, Donna."

Donna sucks in air through her teeth. "Did you raise your voice at that sweet girl, Timber Stag? The poor dear has only been here a week. You know, she doesn't realize you're actually a big softie."

"I am certainly not a 'softie,' Donna," I retort, turning back around in my chair to face her. "But yes. As I said, my tone was out of line. Thankfully, Ms. Jones witnessed my behavior and put a stop to my tirade before I went into closing-argument-mode." I pause, remembering my new associate standing up to me, which was the right call in the moment. "Remind me later to give Juniper Jones my compliments." Donna nods. "How would you recommend I proceed with Ms. Peterson?"

I raise an eyebrow at her, anticipating. I almost never ask for her advice. She generally offers it before I need to. If only all of my employees took the initiative she takes. Juniper Jones takes initiative. She and Donna are the employees I'd take with me anywhere.

"Mr. Stag. Tim. You need to apologize to Alice for losing your temper. And you need to make it count. Sir." Donna raises her eyebrows and nods to me with finality before leaving me alone in my office.

I unwrap the package I grabbed from the cooler with the smoothie. Some sort of nut bar that tastes lightly sweet and chewy. It's miraculously not sticky or crumbly. The perfect texture. From down the hall, I hear the gentle chime of a dinner bell. It sounds almost exactly like the ship's bell my mother had at our house in Highland Park. Before my mother died and my father fell into despair, before my grandmother moved in to save us from becoming destitute as my father drank away his career and my parents' savings. Before I had to manage my brothers and keep us all in school earning top grades to ensure we could all move on to university. That chiming bell takes me back to when I was a different person, and the pain that threatens to surface at these memories is too great. Too much risk here right now.

I dump the wrapper into the trash and grab my bag. Stopping by Donna's desk, I tell her, "I'm going over to the hockey arena to meet with my brother and some of the other players. I'll be gone the rest of the day. Please clear my calendar and reschedule my appointments."

She gives me a disappointed look, but nods. "Will we see you on Sunday?"

"Wouldn't miss it, Donna. See you in the suite."

CHAPTER SIX

Tim

Sunday mornings at the office are my sanctuary. Nobody comes in on Sunday, and I'm totally alone. Granted, I could be working alone from my apartment, but I do my best work in this space I've carved for myself. Something about the view combined with the desk. It opens my thoughts, lets me unpack the depositions, find the key to winning my clients the funds they deserve.

I spent the weekend helping my grandmother around the house. Manual labor helps me work through my frustrations even more than sex. I brushed aside Gran's remarks that she pays people to mow her lawn and change the light bulbs. I remembered my days in high school, mowing lawns around our neighborhood for extra cash toward Ty's hockey fees. Friday night I'd written an email to Alice, apologizing for the way I'd spoken to her and asking her to please make me aware of any future unorthodox arrangements for the office. I thought I'd done a pretty good job, making sure to praise her work so far and reminding her that I valued her contributions to my staff. She really is remarkable. She's done so much in the short time she's been with Stag Law.

Now, after an entire week of distracted work, I feel like I can prepare to crush the coming week. Sundays are a constant promise of a fresh start. A new week. A new chance to seize order. Or something like that. I went for a six-mile run this morning and now I feel really good as I spread out my work along the smooth grain of my desk.

I look at my watch and see I have a few hours of blissful peace before I need to head over to the arena to meet Donna and the rest of the staff in the luxury suite. I dive into the Hawkins file--a contract renegotiation for one of my NFL players--and prepare the entire brief myself. I make a note to take Dawson off this case. It feels good to get my hands dirty with this one. These days, I generally tried to pass off the cut-and-dry cases to my junior associates, but I feel like getting my hands dirty with this one. It might help me regain focus.

I work until I realize I feel ravenous. I forgot to eat after my run. *Shit.* I wonder if Alice left anything around the break room or if she got rid of all the uneaten food for the weekend. As I walk toward the construction zone, I hear a sound that halts me in my tracks.

Alice Peterson is here.

I can hear her singing to herself again. Her voice is clear and strong as she belts out an old Madonna song. I stop in the entrance to the break room, peering around the construction plastic. The contractors had demo-ed the wall and the hall appears transformed just by adding more natural light. There, behind a gleaming stainless steel counter, is Alice. Her wild curls are totally free, splayed around her head like springs. Gone are the shapeless chef whites and clogs she normally wears to work.

Instead, Alice wears black running tights that end just below her knee. Her perfect, round ass is accentuated by the blue light of the open refrigerator as she bends at the waist, taking notes on the contents. I see the white cords of her headphones contrasted against the sheer material of a baggy tank top, the arm holes of which hang open nearly to her trim waist. I suck in my breath at the sight of Alice's sports bra, realizing that the black spandex material is all that keeps Alice's breasts from spilling into my sight. Her pale skin appears nearly white in contrast to the dark material. I long to slide my fingers along the lines of her tiny body, to feel her curves pressed against me.

The room feels devoid of oxygen as I struggle to breathe. She is magnificent. She is every fantasy I've ever had and more and it takes all that I have not to sprint across the room and plunge my cock into her depths. *Jesus, she's fucking gorgeous,* I think. I watch her as she takes inventory. She spins, singing, taking notes, checking everything. She's preparing to crush the week ahead, too. God, she's somehow able to organize everything and manage a thousand little details but still keep this lighthearted attitude about her. I smile as I watch her examine new appliances. This is her realm and, given complete control over it, she has pulled it into order. I like this very, very much.

I'm not sure how long I watch her from the doorway, but suddenly, she stops mid-song and sees me. Alice screams, dropping her clipboard with a clatter. She knocks over a stack of takeout cartons in her haste to pick it up. I dash across the room to help her as her hair tangles with the cord of her headphones.

"I'm so sorry, sir," she mutters. "I didn't realize anyone else was here. Donna gave me a key." At the sound of her mouth calling me "sir," my cock springs to life in my jeans. *Holy fuck* I think. Instead of saying anything, I reach around Alice to gather the food containers. Brushing against her, I feel the smooth skin of her arm begging to be stroked.

I shake my head. She smells lightly of sweat, but also like the earth and sunshine. I smell a thousand different herbs and spices wafting from her and I want so badly to taste her, to dip my tongue into her mouth and sample the flavor of Alice Peterson. "You didn't do anything wrong," I say, standing and putting the containers back on the counter. "I shouldn't have stood spying in the doorway."

She bites her bottom lip and looks away. She finally succeeds at untangling the headphones from her hair and she sets her phone on the counter with her rescued clipboard. I cough uncomfortably and fiddle with the stack of containers, straightening them. "I hope you received my email of apology, Alice."

She snorts, and I'm taken aback. *Was it not a good enough apology?* I try to recall what exactly I'd said to her when I saw her children here in the break room. "Yes, well, I did mean it. I'm truly sorry for the way I spoke to you." I cough again as she nods and doesn't meet my eye.

"Ok, well, I think everything here is set, so I'll see you

Monday, Mr. Stag." She grabs her shoulder bag and moves to walk past me. I'm not ready to be away from her just yet. Panicked, I reach for her.

"Wait," I say, trying to keep my voice calm. "Who is with your children today?"

"*My* children?" She raises an eyebrow and then begins to laugh. I could listen to the sound of her laughter for hours, even if it's at my expense. "You know those are my sister's kids, right? Well, Donna knows that. Because I cleared it with her before I brought them in." She pauses and laughs a bit more. "Woo, that's funny. *My* children. I'll have to tell Amy."

"Your sister's children." I've behaved deplorably. Jumped to conclusions. Badgered the witness. What the fuck is happening to me? I rake my hands through my hair and along my jaw. "Look, Alice, I think we got off on the wrong foot. I want to tell you how impressed I am with what you've done here so far." I gesture around and begin to explain how she's altered the atmosphere at work in just one week. "You're very driven and you're good at what you do," I finish. "We need you here."

She laughs again. "Did you think I was going to quit just because you had a temper tantrum?" She puts her hands on her hips and her violet eyes darken. She's not nervous around me-- quite the contrary. "Did you upset me on Friday? Yes. Was I pissed off? Definitely. But this is a good job and I'd be a fool to walk away just because my boss is a blow hard." She claps a hand over her mouth. "Shit. I didn't mean to say that to you." Her pale skin flames red, from her chest to the tips of her ears, which poke out from among the nest of curls.

"Tell me how you really feel, Alice," I say, smiling. People don't usually speak frankly to me, outside of my family. I'm used to people measuring their words, either because I intimidate them or because they're speaking to me very carefully in a courtroom. "Maybe we are even now?" I suggest, leaning closer to her and boxing her in against the steel counter.

I'm close enough now that I could lean in and kiss her. I could dip my head in toward her plump lips. I'm barely controlling my urge to do just that when she shakes her head. "Nope. Not even.

Your tantrum was in front of my nephews, and I had to explain to them why I work with an angry man who yells."

I'm overcome by this woman. I lean in. *She's not taken, which means she can still be mine.* I know I shouldn't kiss her and I don't think I'm going to. My mouth is an inch from her ear, so I whisper, "I'm sorry I yelled, Alice. I find it very hard to be rational when I'm near you."

I see her eyes scan my body. She meets my gaze and I know she is attracted to me, too. I see her pupils dilate and the pink tip of her tongue licks her teeth before she speaks. "Mr. Stag," she says, "I..." She stares into my eyes and I can feel my chest rising with each breath. I watch her chest rise and fall as she stands inches away from me. I know this is wrong; she's my employee, but she's also the most amazing woman I've ever met. Not only is she fucking gorgeous, but she's a breath of fresh air in this place, and I didn't even realize I was choking until she got here. I start to lean closer. I'm so close to kissing her now, I can feel her warm breath on my face. And then my stomach rumbles, audibly. The mood shifts instantly, the tension melting away as Alice smiles at me.

"You're hungry! Awesome. Let me get you something."

CHAPTER SEVEN
Alice

Holy mother of god, I think as I turn away from my boss to grab some stuff from the new coolers. I was a few seconds away from jumping into his arms. If his stomach hadn't rumbled just now, I probably would have just peeled myself out of my workout clothes and spread myself open here on the counter.

Shit, he looks even hotter in jeans and a hockey jersey than he does in his designer suits. He's still pretty stiff in his weekend getup. His posture. Maybe his dick, too? I put my knuckle in my mouth, telling myself I can't be thinking about his dick. Ever. Maybe I should get him to yell at me again so I stop thinking with my clit and maintain my professional dignity.

"Let me guess," I say. "You forgot to eat breakfast again."

Tim grins and hops up on the counter, sitting beside me as I lay out ingredients. I like this side of him much more than uptight, yelling Tim. "Guilty," he says. "I'm meeting everyone at the arena at one, but I don't think I can make it until then."

I decide I can whip him up a quick omelet since my dad's guys haven't disconnected the old stove. I set to work quickly chopping up some veggies while the butter melts in the pan. "What's going on at the arena today?"

His eyebrows shoot up and I can tell I've said something off. "Shit. Alice, didn't Donna get you a ticket? Fuck."

I shake my head. "Ticket for what?"

He leans in and plucks a bell pepper from my pile as I dump the veggies into the butter to soften. I watch his long fingers bring the food to his mouth and I have to look away from the sight of his lips wrapping around the pepper. He bites and says, with his mouth full, "Today is the first game of the Stanley Cup playoffs. We have a suite for the staff since we represent the--"

"The players union," I finish for him, nodding. "I knew that. I googled you before my interview. My family doesn't really follow hockey. Hey, will your brother play today?" I ask him about the Fury as I whisk the eggs and begin scrambling them in the pan with the veggies. He says his brother Ty will be starting his first game with the Pittsburgh team. I guess that means Juniper will be at the game.

Tim watches me as I make the omelet and says, "I'm truly sorry that you weren't included in the celebration today, Alice. Do you have plans? Can you join us?"

I slide his eggs onto a plate and frown. "I smell like a gym sock and I'm wearing a tank top. I think I'd be pretty cold in a hockey arena," I say, handing him a fork.

I cross my arms in anticipation as Tim takes a bite. His face seems to melt and he says, "Good God, Alice, this is the best omelet I've ever had. What did you do to these eggs?"

I tell him how I used fresh Amish butter from a farm about an hour away and ordered eggs from them, too. "See the color? The yolks are almost saffron. You don't get anything like that at the grocery store." I smile.

I see a vein tick in Tim's neck as he eats, and I'm surprised by how delighted I am that he likes my food. He finishes chewing and says, "I'd really love for you to come with me to the arena, Alice. I'm pretty sure I've got a turtleneck in my office. You could wear that and I'd be happy to get you one of my brother's jerseys. You should probably have a Stag jersey for work purposes, anyway, since he *is* a client."

Holy shit, he's offering to let me wear one of his shirts, I think, wondering if he can see the wet spot I'm sure is appearing in my pants at the thought of slipping his shirt over my head. It would be nice to see everyone from work in a social atmosphere. *What the hell,* I decide, and nod. "As long as you buy me a whisky to warm me up if my legs get cold." And then I feel breathless, because   Tim   Stag   smiles   at   me.

CHAPTER EIGHT

Tim

I try not to think about sitting with Alice Peterson for three hours, knowing she's wearing my shirt. I run to get a black turtleneck from my emergency drawer as she quickly washes the dishes. When I hand her the shirt, I realize it will be comically large on her small body. At six feet, I'm the shortest Stag brother, but I'm still about a foot taller than Alice and a great deal bigger than her all around.

I may not be a professional hockey player like my brother, but I run five miles most days and hit the gym with a merciless trainer whenever I'm not pounding the pavement. I hand Alice the shirt and she laughs. We walk down the hall to the bathroom and I know she's in there changing her shirt. Slipping my shirt onto her smooth skin. I shiver a bit at the thought, but Alice walks out of the door toward me.

She stuffs the tank into her messenger bag and looks around the kitchen, turning off the light. "Should we head over? Are we walking to the arena?"

Dazed, I shake my head and text my car service. "My driver will take us to the VIP entrance," I tell her. "We can stop and buy a jersey for you when we get to the arena." Before I can stop myself, I place my hand on the center of her back to guide her down the hall toward the elevator. I swallow and close my eyes as she stands in front of me, asking questions about the game. When she gives her hair a shake, I'm hit again with the exotic combination of smells that must seep from her pores.

"I'm just going to text my dad and tell him not to expect me later," she says, tapping out a message on her phone. She laughs. "He'll have to fend for himself for dinner. Someone else is going to feed *me* for a change!"

By the time we reach the curb, she's told me about her father and brothers and plumber uncle, all of whom were expecting her to cook them Sunday dinner. I don't feel the slightest bit bad for them, though. I'm about to slide into a car beside her, the smell of limes and ginger--*that's what was in the smoothie,* I think, *fresh ginger!*--hovering around her like an aura of light.

My driver, Joe, looks shocked to see me emerge from the building with a woman. I quickly introduce her as our newest employee, but he gives me a look as he opens the door for her. Joe knows I'm thinking unprofessional thoughts about my corporate chef. I curse the comfortable width of the back seat as Alice slides to the opposite window, which she opens to cheer along with a group of drunken tailgaters as we stop at a red light. "I thought you didn't follow hockey," I say when she finishes shouting 'Let's go, Fury!' like a seasoned pro.

"I might not follow hockey, but I know how Pittsburghers support their home teams," she says. "I'm a Pittsburgh girl, born and raised."

"What neighborhood?" I ask her, curious.

"My family lives on North St. Clair in Highland Park," Alice replies. "I think I told you--or maybe I only started to--you went to high school with my sister, Amy. And one of your brothers graduated with my brother Ryan. From Peabody."

I stare at her, open-mouthed, remembering. I whisper, "The Peterson house. I mowed your lawn for awhile when your mother was sick."

She nods and her face lights with recognition. "Well, I don't actually remember *you* per se, but I do remember my dad hired neighborhood kids to help out for awhile so he and Ry and Dan could spend as much time with mom as we could."

How could I have spent most of my life living a half mile away from this glorious, wild creature and only met her now? We pull in front of the VIP entrance and Joe opens Alice's door.

He grins at me as he catches me staring while Alice walks toward the arena, handing her bag to the security guard to search. "I could get used to this," she says, gesturing around the deserted entry. "No lines! I guess it pays to have a brother on the team," she says.

I shrug and laugh, telling her it's more lucrative to be the team's legal counsel. I try to remember the last time I laughed. The sound takes me by surprise, actually. This woman stirs reactions in me that I haven't felt in years. I've smiled more this week than I can remember smiling…maybe ever. I escort Alice into the pro shop, where we do have to wait in line. I see her notice the price tag on the Stag jersey I grab from the closest rack, but I wave away her protests. "No worries, Alice. This is a work uniform requirement." I smile again. "It'll be a tax write-off, I promise." I slide my Black Card across the sales counter, wondering if Alice will notice it and feel impressed. When she doesn't seem to respond, I am surprised to feel relieved. *Not a gold digger, then.*

The women I usually take out are very much in tune with the Black Card and what it means I can buy for them. Expensive champagne. Dinners that come one, tiny portion at a time on plates drizzled with sauce they won't eat. Alice grabs my arm after sliding the jersey over her head and gasps, pointing across the concourse. "There's a Nakama in the arena! Can I get sushi?"

I assure her she can get whatever she wants in the executive suite and try not to think about how she will look enjoying her food. She swims in the jersey, but I definitely like seeing her with my last name on her back. As we enter the suite, a chorus of cheers rings out. My staff is excited to see her, and I feel a sense of pride mingled with jealousy as she slips away into easy conversation with Juniper and some of the other associates. I chose all of them because they're good at their job, but I almost never interact with them socially. Alice slides among them as easily as if she'd known them for years. I hear her ask about their spouses, and they ask her questions about her siblings. This type of interaction is always so foreign for me. I try to avoid it, so I stand at the back of the room and just watch her. I see Donna looking at me with a raised eyebrow and then I feel myself flush. *What is going on with me?*

I pull aside one of the wait staff and ask them to bring me a sampler platter from Nakama. Then I wait, anticipating the look on Alice's face when I hand her the tray of sushi.

CHAPTER NINE
Alice

I wonder if Juniper can tell that I'm a mess inside. I had to sit as far away from Tim as I could in the car so I would stop throbbing with desire for him. The way he put his hand on my back in the elevator left me breathless, and then walking into the arena on his arm? I need to get it together and remember that I work for him. The kind of women who date Timber Stag are the women who can afford the annual fees on the Black Card I saw him pull out to buy me this jersey.

The announcer lists the starting players, and my co-workers all find seats in the box. Everyone got there before us and already picked the buffet clean, but just as I'm about to ask where I can grab a burger, I feel someone tap my shoulder. My boss is standing behind me holding a tray of what looks like every kind of sushi Nakama makes. I feel my jaw drop and he grins. "Your raw fish and rice, madam," he says.

"You are my hero," I blurt out before I pop a piece of sashimi into my mouth. "I'm starving." I close my eyes--this is delicious. "Mmmm, that's soooo good! I can't believe you bought me sushi. At a hockey arena." Tim nods his head toward two seats in the back row of the box. The seats are amazing--we are looking down right over the middle of the ice and even though we are high up, the glass front of the box retracts until it feels like we are just above the players. "Is that your brother," I ask, pointing to the tall player with shaggy hair and eyes like Tim's. He nods and I can see his pride in his brother as Ty skates a lap around the ice, enjoying the cheers as his name is announced.

And then Tim's arm touches mine on the armrest between our seats and I can't think straight. The blood is pounding in my ears. I keep my head facing the ice, trying to concentrate on the game, wondering if I imagined the heated moment we shared in the kitchen earlier. My skin burns where it's pressed against his and I squirm in my seat as my desire shifts south in my body. And suddenly, the arena erupts as Ty Stag scores a goal just a few minutes into the game.

Everyone around us jumps to their feet, cheering and hugging. I get swept away in the excitement, giving out high fives, and turning to hug the nearest person to me. Who is, of course, Tim. I pull back from the hug and I can barely breathe. I want so badly to be pressed against his body again. His grey eyes are molten and I see him swallow, his Adam's apple rising and falling. I know I'm not the only one feeling the heat.

We sit back down as the game resumes, but Tim keeps his eyes locked on me. I feel his hand move to my knee, those long, strong fingers gently stroking my leg until I whimper, my desire for him magnified by the fact that we are here at his brother's hockey game and there's no way we can do anything. *Can we?*

The light above the goal signals a television timeout, and he leans in. "Come with me," he says. It's not a question, and I nod, following him to a private elevator outside the executive suite. He pulls a key card from his wallet and pushes the button for the conference room. Once we are inside the elevator, I gasp as he pushes me against the wall, pressing his body against mine.

"I want you, Alice," he says, his voice ragged, arms on either side of my face. I can't even get words out, I want him so much. "But I can't do anything about it, because you are my employee." My mind is racing, because I want this so much, and I also know that this would change everything at work.

Or would it? Maybe we just need to do this, savor the experience, get it out of our system. "What if this is just...what if just once..."

"Just once."

I nod and he crashes his lips against mine. I moan into his

mouth, finally digging my fingers into his hair. I feel him bite my lower lip and as the elevator door opens, his hands slide under my ass and he lifts me against his body.

I wrap my legs around his waist as he walks us into the conference room, slamming the door behind us by kicking it shut. I can taste his urgency as he kisses me hungrily. The rough stubble on his cheeks rasps against the skin of my neck as he dips his head, kissing and biting his way down my body and placing me on the edge of the huge conference table.

I start to worry about what this will mean for my job, how I'll ever look at him the same way again at work. But then his hands find my nipples beneath his turtleneck and I stop caring. Tim's thumbs rub my sensitive nubs until they are hard as cherry pits, poking through my sports bra. I moan, loving his ministrations while he continues to kiss the skin along the side of my neck.

I run my hands along his abs, surprised at the rock-hard muscle I feel beneath his shirt. How did I not notice that my boss has the body of an Adonis beneath those tailored suits he wears every day to work? I begin to pull his shirt over his head, desperate to feast my eyes on him. I lick one of his nipples and his eyes fly wide open, meeting mine. He looks wild, unmoored, and I love that I've gotten him to this state.

I pull away from him and begin to peel off my own clothes as he unsnaps his jeans. They slide to the floor and I can see his erection tenting his black boxer briefs. I reach out a hand to touch the impossibly-large bulge and grin, saying, "What have you got for me, Mr. Stag?"

"Jesus, Alice," he hisses, ripping down my running tights and panties in one tug. "Say that again." He pulls my legs so that I'm on the very edge of the table and I lean back on my elbows as he spreads my knees wide.

I am totally bared for him and as I watch him slide down his briefs I see the stiff rod of his cock and I groan. It's huge, and a drop of pre-cum glistens on the tip as he strokes himself. "Fuck me,   Mr.   Stag,"   I   whisper.

CHAPTER TEN

Tim

I have never heard anything as sexy in my entire life as Alice fucking Peterson asking me to fuck her. And she called me Mr. Stag. I hate that this turns me on even more, but my dick has taken total control of my brain by this point.

"Are you on the pill, Alice," I ask as I dip my hand to her sweet center. Her blond curls are as wild below as they are on her head, and I think it's the hottest fucking thing I've ever seen until I look at her face while my fingers spread her slick folds.

She's so fucking wet and her eyes have gone a deep violet as her pupils dilate huge and black. I slide one finger inside her tight, pulsing tunnel and I can barely stand to wait for her answer. "Are you, Alice?"

I stop stroking her and she nods. "Yes. Please, Tim."

Sliding in a second finger, I press the pad of my thumb against her clit. I have to watch her come. I have to see her face when I send her over the edge. She starts to groan and her hips buck up against my hand. Her shirt and bra are rolled up around her shoulders and her bare breasts heave as I stroke her clit. Her head drops back and she screams when I take a taut nipple in my mouth as I start circling her clit faster. I suck on her breasts, which are every bit as soft and round as I imagined. I move between them, using my left hand to heft their weight and press them together while I pump my right hand in and out of her body. I feel her start to squeeze my finger with her pussy and I know she's close. I lift my head from her chest so I can watch her face.

"Come for me, Alice. I want to see you." I never talk this way during sex. I don't know where this is coming from, but as I finish my sentence, Alice erupts. I feel her pussy contract around my fingers and she moans my name again and again.

"Yes! Tim, yes. I'm coming. I'm coming!"

The sound is almost enough to take me over the edge without even sliding inside her, but I have to feel her, and as she finishes the waves of her orgasm, I line up at the entrance to her body and slide inside. Alice gasps as I fill her, but I am beyond consciousness at this point. I'm mad with lust for her and I begin to thrust in and out. Her pussy is liquid velvet against my skin. I've never been inside a woman without a condom before. Never. But fuck, this feels incredible. I lean my weight on my hands, on either side of her head, kissing her sweet mouth again as I set a furious pace.

I hear the sounds of our bodies slamming together and Alice starts moving her hips along with mine. She clings to my shoulders with her soft skin pressed against my chest. I lose myself in the scent of her, the feel of her. As she moans my name again and again I know I'm not going to last. "Alice," I gasp. "Come with me!"

I slide a hand between us, right above the place our bodies are joined, and begin to circle her clit. Then I feel it. Alice's orgasm has her almost convulsing around my dick, and as her tight muscles milk my shaft, I moan her name. "Holy fuck, I'm coming." I feel jets of my heated release fire into her and when it ends, I collapse on top of her on the table, spent.

Panting together, we lie on the table where I've signed multimillion dollar contracts for my clients. A conference room where I'll never again be able to work without seeing Alice Peterson's face as she lost herself and I gave control over to something larger than myself. Whatever happened here was so much more than just fucking.

When I can finally breathe again, I roll off of Alice's body to lie beside her on the table, one hand playing with those amazing breasts. I try to figure out what comes next, because one thing is for damn sure. Fucking Alice once did not get her out of my system.

I already need to make her come again, to watch the pleasure move across her face and throughout her body. There's so much more of her I haven't yet tasted. No--this cannot happen again, and yet I know I need to have her. All of her.

She rolls onto one side and lifts her head onto her bent arm. She smiles at me and says, "That was pretty incredible." I nod and reach behind her head, pulling on her hair tie until her curls fall loose around her face, wild and unkempt and smelling amazing. Her words are muffled through the curtain of hair. "We should probably go back down, though, don't you think? And watch your brother play?" She bites her lower lip and I know she's right, but damn if I'm not already hard again.

Reluctantly, I climb off the table and help her down. We manage to get dressed and into the elevator. When the door opens, I look around, but everyone is back in their seats. I motion for Alice to go ahead of me and I tell her I'll bring her a drink. The reason for our absence will be obvious to everyone if we re-enter together. I hang back at the door to the suite and watch her sit. All I can think about is that Alice has my cum dripping out of her pussy.

CHAPTER ELEVEN
Tim

"You're in a good mood," Donna says when she gets to the office on Monday. I'm not sure how she can tell from across the room until she tells me she heard me whistling from the hallway.

She's not wrong. I feel fantastic. After the game, I asked Joe to drive Alice home since I was meeting my family for the after-party. She, of course, refused the offer and said she was going out with Juniper to celebrate a Fury win. I felt so relaxed after the game that I even agreed to do a shot with my brothers--I rarely drink liquor. I spent too many nights in high school mopping up bourbon-scented vomit when my father stumbled in the door wasted. The smell of it turns my stomach.

But my little brother scored two goals in a Stanley Cup final and I screwed the most beautiful woman I've ever seen in my life. I didn't even get angry when Dad showed up at the club wanting to congratulate Ty. I did have security send him away, though. Fuck him. If he can't be there for our lows, he doesn't get to enjoy the highs.

Donna slides me the folder with this week's priority cases and starts to debrief me, but I cut her off. I'm suddenly starving, both for food and another chance to be near Alice. "Donna, let's put this on hold for a half hour. I'm going to get a muffin."

She smiles and nods. I clap her on the back, adjust my suit jacket, and walk down the hall, feeling only mildly foolish as I check myself in the mirror. *This isn't a date. She works for you. This is...an infatuation.*

I find Alice passing a tray of muffins and juice to a group of construction workers in the kitchen. I feel my inner Neanderthal rising when I notice the way they look at her. One of them is talking to her so familiarly that I want to punch his smug face, until Alice sees me. She smiles and the whole world stops. It's like one of those television moments, where everything else in the room fades away.

Bob the Builder sees me glaring and quickly returns to his work. *Good. Fuck off,* I think.

I walk toward her and she offers me the tray. "Fresh squeezed OJ and bran muffins today," she says. I am dying to know if she thinks about what we did yesterday. If it kept her up all night like it did me. If she is also hopelessly in over her head. Her face doesn't answer any questions, though. Her smile is just the same smile as always.

"Only for you will I taste a *bran* muffin, Ms. Peterson," I say, letting my fingers touch hers when I accept the muffin. I feel that familiar sizzle where our skin meets and she blushes. *I am in trouble,* I decide.

Her eyes hold mine, questioning, and it seems like she's about to say something when I hear a familiar voice say my name. "Tim, yo! This place looks totally different."

I turn around to greet my brother Ty, who is standing in the doorway with our grandmother. My body tenses and I feel my vein tick in my neck. I hate surprises. They know this. "Gran," I say, trying to make my voice sound normal. "What are you two doing here?"

She pushes into the room, touching the stainless steel counters and looking around. "Oh relax, Timber Stag. We're just here for a few minutes." Alice has retreated to her new work area and seems to be busily stirring a fragrant concoction of grains and vegetables. My grandmother takes in the new space and smiles. "I see you took my advice."

Ty has a mouthful of muffin and chews as he looks around. "What the hell did you do here, bro?"

Annoyed, I hand him a napkin and tell them how I've hired a corporate chef, who recommended a kitchen renovation. "Alice

Peterson, this is my grandmother, Anna Stag, and I suppose you have yet to meet my brother Tyrion."

He winks and shakes her hand, waggling his eyebrows suggestively. "Call me Ty, sweetheart." I feel my blood boil and I stare daggers at him, but my grandmother hits him with her purse.

"Stop it, Tyrion. Behave yourself right this instant." He winces and rubs his shoulder as he finishes the muffin. My grandmother beams at Alice. "I'm counting on you to fatten up my grandson," she says. "He doesn't eat enough. He works too hard."

Alice smiles at her and nods, saying, "They all do here! But don't you worry. I've got them all stopping for lunch every day at noon and eating breakfast and afternoon snacks, too."

Alice starts to show my family around the new kitchen, talking about the quinoa salad she's working on for lunch, but I clear my throat. "Gran, Alice has a lot of work to do. I've given her quite a lot of responsibility."

"Well, *Sir,*" my brother says, mocking me, "We're just heading down the hall to sign the forms my new attorney has for my playoff bonus." He grabs another muffin and flashes Alice his most flirtatious smile, and I want to punch him in his smug face as he says, "It was real nice meeting you, Alice Peterson, muffin magician."

She laughs at his joke, and I find myself swimming with feelings, ranging from rage that another guy made her laugh…to pride that she gets along well with my family…back to jealous anger that my sleazy brother is clearly trying to hit on Alice. I'm literally shoving him out of the room and he says, "Ok, ok. Hey, you want to grab dinner with me and Thatcher later? Mad Mex is dark enough that I shouldn't be mobbed by fans on a Monday."

"If I say yes, will you get the hell out of my office?"

"Timber Stag! You watch that mouth, young man," my grandmother scolds, and I mutter an apology. Some things never change.

CHAPTER TWELVE

Tim

Ty is, predictably, late for dinner, but I'm actually glad to get some time alone with my middle brother. He's friendly and outgoing like Ty, only Thatcher is an artist. He's got his own glass studio just north of the city, and he's making a pretty good name for himself in the art world. From what I understand, he's also making good on his goal to screw every single woman in the city. Or at least all the ones who will swoon for his long hair and hipster beard.

Thatcher and I snag a booth in a dark corner and order drinks while we wait for Ty. Thatcher can always tell when something's off with me, and right away he says, "What's got you all messed up, bro? You look like you're about to lose in court."

I exhale, trying to decide how much to tell him. But this is more than a week I've been off my game, unable to focus. Distracted. I was so sure fucking Alice would just get it out of my system, but as the day wore on, and I kept thinking of her with those construction workers, I was more distracted than ever. Not just the idea of them staring at her, but the idea of her bossing them around, making plans. Organizing her space. She's in total control in there, even if her lighthearted demeanor suggests otherwise. "Thatcher…I'm in a predicament."

He laughs and drains his beer, signaling to the waiter to bring us another round. "What's her name, Tim?"

"What makes you think it's a woman?"

"If it was related to work, you'd say, 'this fucking case, man,' and if it was about the family, I'd already have heard about it from Gran." He reaches for the chips and salsa and settles back into the bench. "So tell me about this girl."

"She...distracts me." Thatcher laughs again, and I wish I hadn't said anything. "Fuck you, man. I don't know if a woman has ever gotten in my head like this before." I decide not to tell him her name, that she grew up in the neighborhood, or that she works for me. Instead, I settle on just describing her as someone, professionally speaking, I should not get involved with.

He nods and taps his chips on the table, meeting my eyes. All three of us have the same gray eyes. We got them from our mother. "So you went and got involved anyway, hm?"

"Something like that." I look over my shoulder to make sure Ty hasn't gotten here yet. If he caught wind of my situation, I just know he'd make the association with Alice from earlier. He has a sixth sense for about these things. "It's not just that she's sexy. She's responsible and organized and--"

"Woah." He puts a hand up. "Organized is like porn for you, Tim-bo."

I shake my head. "Thatch, I thought if I slept with her, I'd get her out of my system. You know? Just succumb to the sexual energy and be able to move on with my life?"

"But now you just want her more?"

I exhale deeply. "Yes. Shit, Thatcher, I didn't even use a condom. You know me! I've never in my life slept with a woman without a condom." His eyes go wide at this revelation, because that was something I drilled into all my brothers' heads all through our teenage years. *Do not, under any circumstances, get a girl pregnant. Always cover it up, always. No exceptions.*

"You were like a broken record about that," Thatcher says. "You know, Ty and I used to joke that you were going to become a health teacher and spend your days scaring teenagers away from sex." I drag my hands through my hair, not feeling a bit better after this discussion with my brother. He grins, then, and asks, "So what are you going to do?"

My eyes go wide at this. "I thought you were going to give me advice! What the hell am I telling you any of this for?"

He shrugs, and then kicks my foot, because Ty comes slinking into the booth, looking guilty as sin. Thatcher laughs and throws his arms around both of us. "Ty," he says, grabbing our youngest brother by the chin. "Tell me you at least used a condom?" And all   of   us   break   out   laughing.

CHAPTER THIRTEEN
Alice

Finally, I collapse into the couch when I make it home from the office. It's been two weeks since I slept with my boss, and I've barely had time to think about it. A few days after it happened, one of the baseball players Stag Law represents was arrested for drunk driving with a prostitute in his car. The office has been a mess for ten days--constant frenzied meetings behind closed doors. Everyone is tense. Tim even had to miss his trip to the Stanley Cup final because of a court date.

I've been working long hours, not just to make sure there's food for the Stag Law staff, but Donna explained that we'd be hosting prosecuting attorneys and even city officials, not to mention MLB executives. I've kept the sophisticated fare flowing.

My sister brings me a mug of tea and snuggles up next to me on the couch. I rest my head on her shoulder and sigh as she turns on the *Great British Baking Show*. My favorite. "Did he talk to you today," she asks.

Of course I told my sister what happened during the hockey game. I shake my head. "I didn't even lay eyes on him. I never see him. So it's not like he sees me and acts weird…he's just neck deep in this baseball scandal."

"And how are you feeling about it all?"

"Honestly, I don't know! I still think he's hot as hell, Aim. That was the best sex of my life. Easily. No comparison. But what are we going to do? Fuck once a month and then go about our business? He works around the clock, and he missed his brother's world hockey final...whatever it's called. You know family is the most important thing to me. The *most* important thing." I give her shoulder a squeeze.

"Is Ty upset that he couldn't be there? I mean...when you play sports for a living, maybe it means less if your family can't come to a game. And weren't you a willing participant the last time he missed some of his brother's game? Something about sneaking off and doing the nasty in the conference room in the arena?" She nudges my shoulder and I blush.

I slurp my tea and watch the show, hoping to change the subject. My sister asks me about my menus, and I smile, proud of what I've come up with this week. I did three meals a day for the general staff while offering pastries, herbal tea, and--as Donna requested--calming, comfort food for the big wigs. I'd made everything from savory crepes to strawberry-rhubarb tartlets this week, highlighting local produce. I made simple quiche with ramps, cucumber sandwiches. Fruit salads with mulberries I picked right here in the neighborhood. "Aim, I know you don't know a ton about this stuff, but I did all the ordering, timed it all perfectly, took delivery of the eggs from the Amish farmer for God's sake."

I sigh and she says, "When you talk about your day, you look so happy. I want you to be happy, Al."

"I am happy! I had no idea it would feel this good to fully control a kitchen like this. Maybe I wish things would slow down a little bit."

~~

Three more days pass and I only see Tim when I walk into the conference room to deliver the trays of lunch. He doesn't look up at first, because he's so focused on the paperwork he's reviewing with one of the Stag Law attorneys. Something catches his eye, though, because his head turns to where I'm setting out plates. I smile at him, shyly, and feel myself blush when he returns the smile. He doesn't miss a beat, though, and resumes analyzing the paperwork.

I stop back two hours later to clear everything away and find most of the suits have gone. Tim and his staffer are still at the head of the table, and a man I recognize as one of the MLB executives is seated across from them. I smile and lean in to grab the empty tray and I freeze when I feel a hand on my back.

"Are you the sweet thing who brought us these sweet things?" The MLB suit winks at me, his hand lingering. I freeze. Anywhere apart from work, I'd punch him and tell him off, but I'm very aware that I could jeopardize the company's professional relationship with the professional baseball league. *What a fucking prick,* I think, sliding away from his hand. I'm about to force a smile and duck out of the room when I hear a crash.

I look up to see Tim bursting from his chair, the impact sending it flying into the radiator behind him. "Mitch," his voice is dark and menacing. "Get your hands off--"

Mitch throws his hands up, a smarmy grin on his face. "Woah, woah, easy there. It's been a long day, fellas."

My eyes dart to Tim, who is breathing heavily through his nose, lips pinched into a tight line. Mitch rises and gathers his things, saying, "I think we did all we're going to do for this anyway. I thank you boys and I'll see you tomorrow morning at the courthouse to file the motion."

As he leaves the room, I let out a breath I hadn't realized I was holding. I grab what's left of the trays and head back to the kitchen to clean up. By six o'clock, I can hear the halls are quiet. I'm sitting in my office, bent over my notebook jotting down my thoughts for next week. I'm pretty engrossed in developing a new recipe, because I need to get my mind off that creep. That definitely wasn't the first time some asshole put his hands on me in the restaurant industry. I'm sure it's nowhere near the last, either. But it was the first time I felt like the choice to react to it wasn't my own.

When I worked in the neighborhood restaurant, the owners didn't tolerate that sort of behavior and didn't mind losing a customer if he got handsy and I gave him a piece of my mind. This was a totally different power dynamic. I make a note to talk to Donna about having someone else deliver the food for the conference meetings. Surely there's an intern or something. I don't want to be near those jerks.

I feel my brow furrowed as I try to concentrate. My notes are all over the place. I bury my fingers into my hair, twisting absent-mindedly. I hear someone open my office door, and it startles me. I forgot anyone else was here.

I look up to see Tim, glassy-eyed and disheveled. His tie is loose, and his hair tousled. He leans against the doorframe and just stares at me.

"Tim. Do you want to...come in? Can I get you some water or something?"

He shakes his head slowly but doesn't move. "Alice Peterson," he says, hooking his thumbs into his pants pockets. "I've been...celebrating...our latest victory."

I snort as the fumes reach my desk. It's a small office and he reeks of alcohol. "I can tell." I reach beneath my desk where I've got a case of bottled water. I walk to the door and hand it to him and his fingers linger on mine as the bottle changes hands.

He drops my hand and takes a long pull on the water, leaning his head back against the doorframe. "I fucking hated seeing that fucker's hands on you, Alice. Did you know that?" I nod. He continues. "But then the whole time I was 'celebrating,' I kept thinking. I'm no different from him. I'm not better than him. I'm just some slimeball who fucks his employees."

"Tim, no--"

He scoffs. "I have lost all my control, Alice. All my discipline." He starts tapping his temple with the neck of the water bottle. "I'm distracted. You know what happens when people get distracted?"

I shake my head, starting to worry about him. He must be really drunk. Should I call one of his brothers, maybe? I wonder if he'd give me his phone...

Tim's voice drops to a whisper and he leans close, stroking my cheek. "People get hurt when I get distracted." He swallows and leans his forehead against mine. I've wanted to be close to him like this for weeks, but now I'm not thinking about sex. I'm worried about him. I wrap my arms around him and pull him down into a hug.

"It's ok, Tim."

He shakes his head, but wraps his arms around me. I hear him inhale deeply, feel his hands in my hair as he folds his body down   into   my   arms.

CHAPTER FOURTEEN
Tim

My head is pounding. I crack one eye open and regret it immediately as the room begins to spin. Blinding white light streams through the blinds in my bedroom. *Is this my bedroom?* I take stock of my surroundings. It feels like my bed. Smells like my sheets. *How the fuck did I get home last night?*

This is why I don't drink liquor. I can't be losing entire chunks of my day. I close my eyes again and try to retrace the afternoon. We reached a plea deal and an arrangement with the DA. Then I had that meeting with Mitch from the MLB and he put his fucking hands on Alice.

"Shit. Alice." I clap my hand to my forehead, remembering how I'd gone into her office after I drank most of a bottle of tequila with Ben. The two of us put something like 250 hours into that damn DUI incident over the past two weeks, trying to clear that hotshot pitcher's name as best we could.

I try and dig and can remember nothing after I opened her office door. I take a deep breath and start easing myself out of bed.

There's a glass of water on my nightstand, so I gratefully chug that down, wondering how I thought to leave that there for myself when I got home last night. I see I managed to strip down to my t-shirt and briefs, too. My suit is draped neatly over the clothes rack by my dresser. *What the fuck?*

I stumble into the bathroom and groan as I take the longest piss of my life. And then I freeze mid-stream, my hand leaning against the wall behind the toilet. I hear the sound of footsteps in the living room. Someone is in my apartment.

Panic sets in. Nobody comes up here except my brothers and my grandmother.

What day is it? Is the fucking housekeeper here?

"Tim?" A familiar voice floats down the hall. I shake off my dick and hurriedly stuff it back in my drawers as the bathroom door slowly opens. Alice Peterson is in my apartment, wearing my sweatpants and one of my University of Pittsburgh hoodies.

"Alice? Um, I don't know...I can't--"

She smiles. "Are you feeling ok? I was really worried about you last night." She reaches for my hand and I just stare down at her fingers rubbing mine reassuringly.

"I'm a little hazy on the details." She laughs and tugs on my hand, pulling me into my own kitchen. I settle into a bar stool and Alice gets me another glass of water, explaining that she walked me home.

"Walked? I never walk home," I interject.

"Well, you did last night!" Apparently the doorman took pity on her and let us into my penthouse, since Alice couldn't find my keys and I wouldn't give her my phone. She penguin marched me into the bedroom, got me out of my suit, and made sure I passed out on my side.

"I hope you don't mind, I borrowed some clothes," she says, gesturing to my gear. *As if I can ever wear them again and not think about her white skin inside them.* Outwardly, I just shake my head. "I crashed in your guest room," she says. For the first time, I'm glad my realtor convinced me to get a two bedroom. And for the millionth time, I'm relieved my housekeeper keeps everything magazine-spread-ready at all times. Alice starts to walk down the hall, saying something about how she will strip the sheets and get them started in the washer, but I move, as quickly as I'm able with my aching head, to stop her.

"Alice, don't even think about it." Her eyes meet mine, questioning. "Thank you. Thank you for taking care of me." I pause. "This isn't...usual for me. I don't ever..." I give up and run my hands through my hair again. "Can I buy you breakfast?

It's the least I can do."

She shakes her head, looks at her watch. "I really should get back home before my family wakes up," she says. "It's only 7 now, so I might make it if my nephews don't come crashing downstairs." She laughs, and I decide that's the only sound in the world that doesn't hurt my head.

She agrees to let Joe drive her home, at least. I don't think I am sober enough to drive yet. *Jesus.* I can't be doing shit like this, letting myself lose control. After I call the car for Alice, I crawl back in bed and don't emerge until it's nearly dark.

~~

The next day, my brothers and I all meet to go for a jog in Highland Park before brunch with our grandmother. The three of us don't say much, but it's nice to run together with them. We strip our shirts after the first lap around the path and Ty picks up the pace. He knows we can't fully keep up with him, but the rest of us aren't too shabby considering he's a pro athlete. He throws a grin over his shoulder and tears off, and we scramble to chase after him as he shouts "I thought you fuckers were out for a run today? This is like mall walking!" Before long, we are sprinting through the park, trading obscenity-laced digs at each other depending on who's able to pull ahead. After five miles or so, we stop for a drink at the fountain by the reservoir. Our chests are heaving, but my brothers are ok. I like us like this, together, and I like seeing our family tattoo--we all have a stag etched onto our chest, leaping over a field of laurel. That was our mother. Laurel. Thatcher designed the tattoo and we all went together on Ty's eighteenth birthday. Of course, Thatcher now has about a hundred more tattoos since he's an artist and all.

Ty spits a mouth-full of water at me, and that tips off a three-way wrestling match. Suddenly, we are all kids again, just rolling in the grass until we don't feel like fighting anymore. I give my younger brother's shoulder a final punch, saying, "It's good to have you back, baby brother."

"Wasn't such a baby when I was kicking your ass a few

minutes ago, was I, big brother?"

Thatcher's stomach rumbles and reminds us all that we're starving after that workout. Arm in arm, we walk down the hill toward our childhood home. My thoughts drift, as usual, to Alice. The way she took care of me like that, without being asked, like it was no big deal. She's always taking care of her family. She works her ass off and then goes home and takes care of her dad and nephews. I never met anyone as caring and kind as her. It all just comes to her naturally, not an act or with an ulterior motive. What would it be like, I wonder, to have her waiting for me with breakfast. I try to stop myself from imagining her in my kitchen again, cooking for me and only me. Naked. *God, I've never even seen her fully naked.*

Gran has pancakes and bacon ready for us when we finally walk in the door. Ty opens the fridge and begins chugging orange juice right from the carton, and the rest of us berate him as my Gran smacks him with her spatula. I grab my youngest brother in a headlock and pull him down, rubbing a knuckle playfully into his hair. Again, though, my mind shifts to Alice Peterson and her pink, plump lips. What I wouldn't give to twist my fingers through her hair again.

We sit down to eat, and nobody speaks for the first few bites while we inhale Gran's perfect pancakes. Thatcher pauses, though, and says, "These taste a little different, Gran. Did you do something new?"

She nods, smiling wide at his observation. "I knew you would be the one to notice," she says, pinching his cheek like he's still ten years old. "I added almond extract and a dash of cinnamon." We all moan appreciatively, shoving more of the pancakes in our mouths. "Alice was giving me pointers."

I nearly choke on my food and Thatcher starts pounding on my back. "Who the hell is Alice?"

Gran rolls her eyes and he apologizes for swearing. "She's the chef I told Timber to hire," Gran says.

Ty just nods knowingly. "The muffin girl. Right on." I don't like the way he grins at me. He knows something.

Feeling worried they can read my thoughts, I take a deep

breath and remind myself there's just been the one indiscretion. Well…and the fact that she took me home blackout drunk Friday night. Which they would have no way of knowing. I take a long drink of OJ and ask my grandmother when she was trading cooking secrets with Alice. Gran starts cleaning up, and I rise to help her as she talks. "Well, I thought she looked awfully familiar when I saw her at your office the other day, and then I remembered! The Peterson family lives over on St. Clair. Timber, don't you remember? You mowed their lawn for awhile when her mother was sick, the poor dear." My grandmother hands me plates as I silently load the dishwasher. "Well wasn't I out for a walk the other evening and saw her playing with her nephews in the park? She recognized me right away and we got to talking. That's all."

Thatcher catches me staring slack-jawed as Gran walks out of the room, muttering about what a nice girl Alice is and how good neighbors make the best friends. He furrows his brow and says, "Your face right now leads me to believe that this Alice chick might be the 'distraction' you mentioned." He looks at me, expectantly.

I choose not to say anything to my brother, but I toss on my t-shirt and walk out the back door, heading through the alley toward   St.   Clair   Street.

CHAPTER FIFTEEN
Alice

"Whose birthday is it again, Aunt Alice," my nephew Eli asks, his mouth full of cake batter.

I wipe a stray drop of the chocolate batter from his cheek and tell him, "June 30 is Linda Day. My mom--your mom's mom, too--was Linda, and we celebrate her birthday every year to remember her and talk about how much we love her, even though she's not here with us." It's hard for a five year old to grasp, but today is a big day for my family.

My brothers are both here, wearing nice pants and clean shirts for a change. We all get takeout from Mom's favorite barbecue place and every year, I bake her favorite cake. Rich, flourless chocolate cake pairs nicely with fresh raspberries this time of year. My sister took the boys out wandering to pick some in the wild along the trails in Highland Park yesterday.

I'm about to slide the cake into the oven when I hear a knock at the front door. "Ry!" I shout to my brother. "Can you get the door? I think that's the food."

He walks to the front door with my nephew Ethan slung over one shoulder and I hear him fling the door open. As I shut the oven, I look up to see the dour face of my boss standing on the front mat.

I freeze, and Ryan crumples his face. "You're not the guy from Showcase." He pauses a beat, assessing Tim, who looks like he's just come from an intense sweat session. "Can I help you?"

Eli runs over to his brother and uncle and points at Tim. "That's the angry man from Aunt Alice's work! The one who yells!" Tim's cheeks flush and I walk over to try to salvage the situation.

"Ry, this is my boss. Do you remember Tim Stag? Aim said he went to school with you all. Grew up in the neighborhood."

Ryan nods as he lowers my nephew to the ground. "Stag. I think so. What's up, man? You need something?"

I've never seen Tim at a loss for words. At work he's always so confident. In total control. Except when he was yelling at my nephews I guess. *And when he dragged me off into the conference room for sex...*at the memory, my own face flushes. "Tim," I say, "Come inside for a drink of water?"

He seems mortified and lingers in the doorway. "I don't know what I was thinking," he says, quietly. "I was at my grandmother's house for pancakes and she said she saw you and..."

He drifts off, looking around at my extended family. Dad, Dan, and Doug are watching the baseball game on TV and my sister is flitting around setting out plates and napkins. The actual delivery guy starts climbing the porch steps, and Ryan sort of shoves Tim into the house as he squeezes past to pay for the food. Tim looks into my eyes. "I'm interrupting something here. I'll just see you tomorrow, Alice."

"Wait!" I shout, before thinking twice. "Please stay."

He looks as if I've asked him to lend me a kidney, but he enters the house. "Everyone," I shout above the normal family chaos. "This is Tim and he's here for ribs."

My brother and brother-in-law don't turn from the TV, but my dad glances up. "Stag!" he says, waving. "Good to see you again, son. You still over there on Euclid Ave?"

Tim nods. "Yes, sir. My grandmother lives there, although I own it now." He pauses and looks at me. "I'm not sure why I said that last bit."

I pat his arm and tell him to have a seat on one of the bar stools. I slide him a glass of water, saying, "There's just a few minutes left until the cake comes out of the oven, then we'll eat while it cools." I smile at him. It's good to see him, to be near him, no matter what the circumstances.

He waves around at my family as my nephews start firing Nerf darts at him. "What is all this?"

As I explain Linda Day to Tim, I see his face shifting. His emotions are all over the place as he listens to me explain. I know that his mother is gone, too. I lean closer to ask him, "How does your family remember your mom?"

His face is ashen and stiff. He shakes his head and his mouth moves a bit, but no sound comes out. Finally, he whispers, "we don't speak of her. Ever." Suddenly I'm overcome with sadness for him. For all the pent up grief he must carry. I know his brothers are gregarious and friendly. I'm so sad for them that they don't share their feelings about their lost mother, even to remember what they loved about her. I walk around the counter and wrap my arms around Tim. He melts into my chest and I see my sister Amy looking at me strangely, but I don't feel like worrying about her right now.

Tim is breathing fast and heavy, and I rub his back until the timer beeps on the oven. Reluctantly, I break our embrace to pull out the cake. He props his elbows on the counter, head in his hands. My sister calls everyone to the table to eat and I touch Tim's shoulder. "Come join us," I say. And he does.

CHAPTER SIXTEEN

Tim

The Peterson family goes around the table sharing remembrances of their lost mother. Even the little boys, who never met her, have something to say about things they've learned about Linda. By the time we're done with cake, I feel like I knew her, too, even though all I did was mow their grass as a teenager. When it came to be my turn, I was stunned when Alice's father reached for my hand and thanked me for helping around the yard so they could get more time with Linda in the hospital. I almost lost my shit and wept right there with them.

This family is certainly different from mine. I vacillate between sorrow and rage when I think about how my mother's death is the great taboo at our house, and my father's drunken absence is the elephant in the room. *Why don't we ever just sit and talk about it like this?*

I think Alice can tell that I need to escape, because she dabs her mouth with a napkin and tells the table at large, "I'm going for a walk with Tim. Don't any of you dare use a scouring pad in my springform cake pan when you're washing the dishes." There are groans and laughter and one of her brothers throws a napkin at her as she tugs on my hand and leads me toward the front door.

My dick twitches in my pants as a reminder that no matter what is going on in my world, my lust for Alice Peterson trumps all. We walk in silence for a few blocks until she says, "I'm really glad you came by today."

I clear my throat. Why does she make me so nervous? "I wanted to thank you again for your discretion and your assistance the other night."

She smiles. "You know," she says, playfully tugging on my shirtsleeve. "You talk in your sleep a bit. At least when you're drunk."

"Not true," I counter, playing it cool while I inwardly panic.

She nods. "You said, and I'm not paraphrasing, 'pretty Alice, hairy curls. Just want to touch them all the time.'" And she laughs. The sound is so warm and delightful I can't help but feel at ease with her.

"Well," I say, "all of that is true." And she flushes. I grab her hand and pull her toward a bench in a nearby bus shelter. We sit, a bit stiffly. My voice is a harsh whisper as I confess, "I'm wild about you, Alice, and I can't seem to stop thinking unprofessional thoughts."

She looks up at me, her violet eyes liquid and warm, and says, "I think terribly unprofessional thoughts about you, too." And I bury my fingers in her curls as she rests her head on my shoulder. We sit in silence for a long time until she asks me about my mother.

Nobody ever asks about my mother. I swallow the bile that rises in my throat when I think about her death, but I remember how much lighter Alice's family seemed in talking about their own worst moments. I choke out, "I missed the bus. I got distracted at the library and missed the bus. I called from the payphone and she dashed out in the rain to come get me." Alice grabs my hand and starts gently rubbing my palm. "We were supposed to have my grandmother over for dinner that night, so she was in a rush to get me and get back to her pot roast."

I pause, and Alice looks up to my eyes. I've never told this to anyone before. She kisses my forehead and I close my eyes. "You can tell me, Tim. I know how it feels."

I shake my head. "Not this. You don't know how this feels. She was t-boned on 5th Ave. Two blocks from the library. Someone was driving the wrong way in the bus lane and she went to turn left as whoever it was kept plowing ahead straight into her." My words catch in my throat, but I keep talking. "After an hour or so passed, I decided just to walk home. Two miles in the rain, I stewed and steamed that she would do this to me. I thought she was teaching me a lesson about missing the bus. I slammed the front door, ready to scream at her. My family sat around the living room in the dark, just staring. My brother Thatcher whispered to me that she'd died instantly in the crash."

I haven't cried for my mother in probably 15 years, but I just begin to release a torrent of years of grief. I'm not sure how long I cry onto Alice's shoulder, but I know she holds me and strokes my back, whispers into my ear to let it out.

"You were a kid, Tim," she soothes. "Kids miss the bus. Adults miss the bus." I'm shaking my head against her shoulder. Alice says, "Tim. The only person at fault here is the jerk driving the wrong way in the bus lane. Not you. Not you, Tim."

I don't know how long she repeats this phrase. When I finally become aware of my surroundings, Alice is gazing into my eyes. Her hands are everywhere on my shoulders and arms and, no matter what I try, I can concentrate on nothing apart from the scent of her. I can tell that she senses the shift in my mood because she gently rubs my jaw with her thumb.

"I like it when you look scruffy like this," she says as the tip of her digit rasps against my two-day stubble. I turn my cheek so it brushes against her palm and when I hear a breathy sigh escape her throat, my dick jumps to attention.

I can't bear to not be kissing her, and I dive into her mouth, tasting the chocolate sweetness of cake as my tongue delves into Alice's warm depths. I move both hands into her wild hair--has it been down and free this entire day?--knotting my fingers into the blonde tendrils. I feel her come alive in my arms, returning the intensity and desperation of my kiss. My mind races--how can I get her to my apartment? Where can I take her to peel her out of those clothes?

Someone clears their throat and Alice leaps from my arms. An old man with a cane is standing near the bus shelter, gesturing. "Mind taking that elsewhere so I can wait for my bus in peace?" he asks, his mood somewhere between amused and irritated.

Alice mumbles an apology and starts down the street back toward her house. I follow, cursing the old man who stole my moment with Alice. When we get to her porch, she moves to enter the house and I reach for her hand. "Wait," I say, and she looks at me expectantly. I am so lost around this woman, unraveled. She's opening up pieces of me I don't understand. "Let me take you out to dinner. To thank you for taking care of me the other night."

Suddenly I feel nervous, like a teenager asking his first crush to the dance, I suppose. For the first time, it matters to me that a woman agrees to my plea. "I'd love to take you somewhere and let someone else do the cooking for you."

Alice breaks into a smile, and I feel my whole body relax. "Thank you, Tim. That sounds really nice." She reaches for my hand and gives it a squeeze before releasing it. My skin vibrates with anticipation and nerves. I run a hand through my sweaty hair, remembering that I'm a mess. An actual mess. God, I walked over to her house and interrupted her family, caked in sweat.

"Saturday night, then, Alice? Where should we go?"

Alice begins babbling in that delightful way she has about her, unfiltered. This was probably the best question I could have asked. "Ooh! Morcilla is supposed to be amazing," she says, "Do you like Spanish food? But Legume is so nice...oh, or could we eat at Spoon? Or Cure! Do we have to wait until 8 to eat? I don't understand why people do that. I get hungry early. Wait." She puts a hand on my arm again as I laugh, enjoying her excitement. "How will you get a reservation any of those places for Saturday?"

Now I can return to my sense of confidence and control. "Alice," I tell her. "I work with sports stars. When a Stag calls a restaurant, we get a table."

"Well look at you," she says, teasing. "In that case, I pick Cure."

CHAPTER SEVENTEEN
Alice

My family all stares at me when I walk back inside the house. They're sitting around watching old movies, and my sister leaps up and pulls my arm. "Alice," she hisses, dragging me into my bedroom. "You tell me everything this instant."

I flop down on the bed and tell her all of it, how Tim opened up to me about his mother and that kiss we shared on the bench. "Amy, it was...I've just never been kissed like that before."

She throws open my closet and puts her hands on her hips. "We have to go buy you something to wear for next weekend, or you won't get kissed like that again."

"Shut up, jerk," I say. But she's right. I've spent the last years waitressing, cooking, or playing with my nephews. I haven't bought a new dress in ages. Tim is always so put together, dressed in killer suits. I think about how young he is, how young he was when he started taking care of his family. He has to look like a shark in a world of salt and pepper suits who've been in the game for decades. Dress for the job you want, I guess they say. Right now, the job I want is Tim Stag's sex goddess. Giggling, Amy and I leave the house and drive to the mall, where she forces me toward the more expensive department stores.

"Alice, you're going out with Tim Stag. You can't look like you're headed to a hockey game this time." She reminds me of my higher-than-expected salary and I agree to try on a beautiful, cobalt blue dress by Kate Spade. My sister pushes me toward the low-cut, slinky dresses, but that's just not my style. She rolls her eyes at me when I tell her I'm going with the sleeveless, boat-neck dress. "I guess he already knows he can get the milk for free," she says. I remind her that it's at least shorter than I feel comfortable with and we find a pair of strappy heels to go with it.

At work the next day, I'm not sure how things will go when I see Tim, but he stops by the kitchen for breakfast and I feel butterflies in my stomach just looking at him. He lets his finger linger on my hand when he takes a muffin from me, and I bite my lip, wondering how I will make it until Saturday before really touching him again.

I think he's very busy with a lot of hockey endorsement contracts now that the season is over, because I don't see him much all week. I hear Juniper talking about him taking his grandmother to some doctor appointments even though Ty is the one who lives with her right now. I really like that Tim makes sure his family is ok, in his own way.

I'm like some teenager in middle school, looking for him every few minutes, unable to speak when I do see him, finding ways to make sure I touch him. I spend the entire week on edge, on fire, constantly aroused and remembering the feel of him inside me, around me, kissing me. Friday afternoon, as I'm cleaning the kitchen up for the weekend, I hear someone approach from behind, and I know it's him before I even turn around.

"I was starting to think you were avoiding me," I say, continuing to wash the dishes. I've got all the food put away and I couldn't stand to be in my chef coat for another minute today, so I'm washing dishes in my tank top. Most people have gone home for the weekend already and it's been a long, hot day in the kitchen. Despite the heat, I shiver when I feel Tim's hands on my skin.

His breath is sweet against my cheek as he says, "I have, Alice. I can't concentrate when I'm near you." I swallow, relieved it's not just me overcome by attraction. Not just me imagining something that's not there. He starts to stroke my arms and I let the dish drop into the soapy water. I lean against the sink, unable to move.

"What's happening, Alice? Why can't I be near you without needing to touch you like this?" He presses his body into my back and I feel the heat of his body radiating through his tailored suit. I let my head drop back against his chest and a small moan escapes my throat when his fingertips graze against my breasts. His voice is barely audible, whispering, "I thought once I fucked you, that I could go back to normal. But I can't get enough of you." His breath is ragged and then his lips gently swipe the skin behind my ear. I shiver against him.

"Tim," I say, my voice shaking, "I want you, too." I suck in a great gulp of air and turn to face him. "But not like this. Not here at work."

He frowns, but keeps his hands on my arms. "Tim, I'm serious." I extract myself from his grasp and immediately miss his warmth, his touch. "What will everyone else think? This job is very important to me. My work as a chef is very important to me."

"Alice, I don't think my staff will like your cooking any less just because we're--" he stops mid-sentence.

"What are we, Tim? What is this?"

His face hardens and he runs a hand through his hair, but doesn't answer.

"You're distant and...and bossy at work, but then you pour your heart out to me. You come to me drunk after a stressful day at work and I just--"

"You make me feel safe." He doesn't look at me, but reaches for my hand. He strokes the skin of my palm. "I don't have to take care of you, Alice. And I want you." He brings my hand to his mouth, gently licks my palm in a way I feel straight through to my core. "Very." Lick. "Very," he licks my wrist. "Badly."

I feel my heart racing when he finally meets my eyes. I remember his grandmother telling me how he's always taken care of his brothers, how his father fell apart when their mother died and Tim became the man of their family, even though he was only a teenager. Tim kept his brother in private school even when he got suspended for fighting--got Ty to focus on hockey where it was safe to let out his aggression. Tim always knew what everyone in his family needed, and now he says I am what *he* needs? "I make you feel safe? Me?"

He nods, still stroking my palm with his thumb, leaning against the steel counter with his other hand. I see that he's loosened his tie, that he needs a shave. I like when he looks disheveled like this. "Come home with me, Alice," he says, tugging me closer. And oh my, but he smells good. And feels good. Our romp in the conference room was so fast...what would it be like to spend the entire night with this man?

And then I remember. "I can't tonight," I tell him. "I told Juniper I'd hang out."

"Juniper *Jones?*" He seems incredulous, but I nod.

"We're friends. She's nice. We're going kayaking." I start babbling again, telling him how Juniper wants me to get as excited as she does about exercising.

Finally, Tim presses a finger to my lips and says, "All right then, Alice. I'll have to wait until tomorrow." I nod. "I'll pick you up at 6," he says, and I don't exhale until I've watched him walk around the corner.

I change in my office and walk down the bike path to meet Juniper, who has already rented a kayak for us. "You know I'm a total beginner, right?"

She smiles. "I know this isn't the Olympics, Alice. You climb up front."

Juniper steers and we slowly make our way up the river, past the baseball stadium. It's pretty cool to watch the sunset from this vantage point on the river. She starts to tell me all about how she got into rowing, how her dad was even an Olympic champion. "Rowing is basically all I have now," she says, "apart from you of course." She splashes me with her paddle.

"Come on, June. The river water is gross. And of course you have me! You were my first friend at Stag Law." Juniper explains that she caught her boyfriend with another woman and needed a new job, a new place to live. Ben from work is the brother of one of Juniper's teammates from Boston. "That's so cool how the rowers just hook you up like that. They sound like family."

"They're absolutely a family. My only family now that my dad is gone."

I smile, thinking about how I keep surrounding myself with people who understand how important it is to stick together and support your family, no matter how that family is defined. "Hey June?"

"Yeah, Al?"

"I hate this."

She laughs and we head back to the dock. Arm in arm, we walk to get Thai food while I tell her about my ideas for work next week. By the time I get home, I've completely forgotten to be nervous about my date tomorrow. I'm tired out from kayaking, and I drift quickly to sleep, remembering the feel of Tim's touch on my sore arms.

CHAPTER EIGHTEEN
Tim

I consider using my driver, but decide I don't want anyone else looking at Alice today. It's been awhile since I've taken my Volvo XC90 for a ride, anyway, and I like the look on Alice's brother's face when I pull up at the Peterson house. "Nice ride, Stag," he says.

"Safest car on the road," I tell him, reaching behind the driver seat to grab the flowers I got for Alice.

"I know that, asshole," he says. I shrug, straighten my collar, and adjust the flowers. Her brother nods, approving, and steps aside as I walk toward the door. I'm about to knock when he grins and shouts through the open porch window.

"Yo, Alice! Your *date* is here!"

I feel very much like I'm picking up a prom date when I see Alice's nephews scramble into the living room and press their faces against the picture window. But then Alice comes outside and all other thoughts slip from my head.

"Shit, Al, you clean up nice." Her brother is the king of the understatement, apparently. Alice is radiant. My eyes follow the blue line of the dress from her collarbones to where it stops mid-thigh, not far enough below her ass. Alice's legs look amazing in the strappy heels she wears that bring her closer to chin-height than her usual stop at my shoulder.

I clear my throat when she catches me staring and offer the flowers. "Dahlias," I say. "To match your eyes." When she smiles I forget her entire family is standing around watching. I feel my cock spring to life in my pants and cross my hands in front of my body as Alice turns to put the flowers in water.

She lets me put an arm around her as we walk toward the car. "Ooh," she says. "Is this one of those Volvos where the front seat can be a baby seat?"

I cock my brow, impressed that she would know that, but she reminds me that her brother works as a mechanic. "Ry wanted my sister to get one of these when my nephew was born," Alice says. "But it was a bit outside their price range."

I smile and open the door for her, letting my eyes linger on her legs as she climbs inside. "Worth every penny if it keeps you safe," I tell her, pleased to see her sink into the white leather interior. Someday, I vow, I will fuck Alice Peterson in this car.

I drive to the restaurant and she tells me about kayaking with Juniper. "My arms are sore today," she says. "Which is surprising because I work with my hands all day, you know?"

"I'll rub them for you later," I tell her, sliding my hand from the gearshift to her knee. When she doesn't resist, I decide to keep my hand there until I need to shift gears at a red light.

"How did you get this car with a manual transmission," she asks, running her hand along the dash.

I shrug. "I imported it."

"You imported a manual transmission Volvo whose front seat converts into a baby seat?" She looks skeptical.

I turn to look at her, returning my hand to her knee and regretting the manual transmission for the first time, since it means I frequently have to move my hand. "It's the safest car in the world, Alice."

She puts her hand on mine and smiles. I'm almost disappointed when we arrive at the restaurant and I have to break contact with her to hand the keys to the valet. The hostess greets us warmly as we enter--she wasn't so friendly on the phone when I said I was coming in with just a few days' notice, but I see that she's guiding Alice toward a private table.

"Welcome to Cure. Mr. Stag informed us that you'd be having the tasting menu," she says to Alice, a bit woodenly, handing Alice a card describing the six courses and their drink pairings.

Alice is radiant, and not just because she's dressed to kill. Her joy in reading over the menu is infectious, and soon Alice is explaining pickled pears and violet mustards until I'm actually excited about my food for once.

"You should come with me to all my restaurant meetings," I tell her. "I'm usually so busy persuading the client that I barely pay attention to what I'm eating."

She scoffs. "If you come to places like this and manage not to focus on your food, I'm not sure there's any hope for you in this world."

The server arrives with our first round of drinks and I raise my glass to Alice, saying, "You give me hope for a lot of things, Alice." She tries to hide her flush behind her wine glass. "You must have noticed by now that I don't really trust very many people. I've been so impressed with how you approach your work."

Alice picks up her oyster and tells me to look at it closely. "Food," she says, "is so much more than a group of ingredients hanging out together. It's a family. It functions best *together*." She gently prods the sauce with her finger. "If you leave out a detail, an ingredient, a step in the preparation process, it all falls to pieces. But together..." Alice slides the oyster into her mouth and, watching her swallow, I feel my pants tighten around my growing bulge. "Together, it's perfection." She reaches across the table to feed me *my* oyster and I don't think anyone has ever done anything to turn me on more. "I've always just been able to see how all the details need to come together," she says and shrugs. "It's because my family has always focused so much on working   together   for   the   big   picture."

CHAPTER NINETEEN
Alice

By the time we reach the dessert course, I'm tipsy on the excellent wine and Tim's intense attention. He's so direct as he tells me how much he admires everything from my work ethic to the ways my family gets along with each other...and how much he wants me. If only he knew how much that feeling is mutual! I notice that his cheeks are dark with stubble--he must have to shave twice a day if he has evening meetings--and I can see the vein in his throat pulse above the collar of his button-down shirt.

As he pays the check and calls for the valet, I'm feeling ready to just pull him into a dark alley to have my way with him. He's so confident in this environment, telling people what to do and expecting that they'll respond immediately. Which, of course, they do. I can tell the hostess hates that I'm going home with him. Her jaw is clenched when I smile at her, but her whole face warms when Tim tells her he'll be sure to come again soon with Stag Law's top clients.

The valet pulls up with Tim's Volvo, and Tim's hand lingers along my back as he opens the door and helps me inside. His skin leaves a trail of sparks up my back. "Where to now," I ask him as he slides into the driver's seat.

"Now, Alice, I'm taking you back to my apartment to fuck you properly."

"Oh," I say. Then I nod. I barely breathe the entire car ride. He slides into a spot in the garage and pulls me into the elevator. His mouth claims mine, his rough stubble rasping along my skin as he drags kisses along my collarbone. One hand slams the Penthouse button on the elevator while the other pulls me tight against his body. "I don't want anyone to see," I plead as his fingers sneak up the back of my skirt.

He growls against me, sliding his tongue into my mouth in response and I forget to worry about it. We tumble into his apartment and he picks me up, carrying me down the hall toward the room I last saw when I half dragged him to bed. *God, was that only a week ago?*

He throws my purse on the dresser and starts unbuttoning his shirt. I stand next to the bed, panting, and watching him undress. I am so eager to see all of him. Last time was so frenzied. I felt but couldn't admire the perfection he hides under those tailored, designer suits. Tim's muscles are long and lean and hard. The perfect V of his lower abs is hidden by the waist of the pants he stops unbuttoning. Tim walks toward me and says, "Turn around, Alice."

I immediately comply, and moan softly as his fingers tease the back of my neck. He gathers and lifts my hair, searching for the zipper to the dress. Painfully slowly, he eases it down and I feel the halves of my dress peel open. "God, Alice, you are exquisite," he says, running his hands along my skin. I feel the heat of his body against my back and I gasp as he lowers the dress and my panties in one short tug.

He turns me around and I reach for his pants. My body yearns to be pressed against his, fully naked. He dips his dark head and takes my nipple into his mouth through the material of my bra. His tongue swirls around the needy peak and I think I've never felt anything as nice as this. My hands find purchase in Tim's boxers. I wrap my fist around his hardness, loving the smooth length of him in my hand. He continues his work teasing my nipples until I can't stand any longer.

We tumble backwards onto his bed. He feels so good lying on top of me. So solid. I move my hands to his chest, loving the powerful feel of him. Tim starts to rub his cock against my seam and I cry out. He smiles and holds my gaze, teasing me slowly.

Each time I'm on the edge of exploding, he backs off, returns to my nipples. "Tim, let me come. Please!"

I beg him, desperate for release. But he shakes his head. His voice is low and I feel his chest rumble as he says, "I want you to come around my cock, Alice. I want to feel your pleasure." I sigh as he slides into me. "You're so wet, baby."

"You turn me on so much," I tell him, but then I lose my ability to speak. I wrap my legs around his waist and the angle is just right. My clit rubs against Tim as he thrusts deep inside me again and again until I'm tumbling over the edge. My orgasm rolls through my whole body in waves. He teased me for so long, my entire body is on fire. I thrash and claw at his chest, screaming his name for an eternity.

"Fuck, Alice," he says, looking into my eyes. "You are so sexy. This is so hot." He rests his forehead against mine, keeping me still, and after a few more hard thrusts, I feel him spill inside me.

My bones have turned to jelly. I'm practically purring as Tim slides out and pulls me against his body. I hear him murmuring soft words to me as he strokes my arm, but I'm too overstimulated, high in the afterglow of a mindblowing orgasm. I drift off into a deep sleep curled against his body.

CHAPTER TWENTY
Tim

I don't want to move. I'm holding perfection here in my arms, in my bed. I've never brought a woman to my apartment before, never wanted to stick around after I've fucked someone. But I don't ever want Alice to leave my bed and I can barely wait to be inside her again, to move with her and give her pleasure. I know that I've completely unraveled for this woman. All my rules are broken. All my composure is gone and somehow, with my fingers twined through her mad hair and my body pressed against her soft curves, I just don't care.

Alice has fallen asleep in my arms and it feels so right. After awhile, I hear her phone chirping inside her purse on my dresser. Some sort of persistent alarm grows louder, and I don't want it to wake her. I slip out of the bed to reach for it. The words "Little blue boys!" flash across her lock screen as the tinkling bells keep chiming. I figure she must have planned to tuck her nephews in or something, so I turn it off and climb back into the bed beside her.

As I wrap my naked body against hers, she stirs. I love the tiny noises she makes, the contented sighs as she wakes. I grow hard as Alice wiggles her bottom. *Time for round two,* I decide. "Hey, you," Alice says when I start kissing her shoulder. I let my hand fall to her breast and am rewarded with a soft moan as I massage her nipple. "How long was I asleep?"

"Just a few minutes," I tell her, continuing my exploration of her creamy skin. She turns her head to kiss me and I'm lost to her. I pull her close against my body, the swell of her ass against my cock. She lifts one leg a bit to give me access to her center, and I slide home. We fit together so perfectly. "Alice," I whisper. "You're so wet. You feel so good."

"Mmmm." She groans into my mouth, moving with me. I know I'm not going to last long. This feels too intense. I drop a hand to her clit and, using the pads of two fingers, find the rhythm that will drive Alice over the cliff. She moves with me, thrusting her hips against my hand.

I'm so close to losing control, but I need Alice to come first. "Now, baby. Let go!" And she does, moaning and thrusting until I can't help but join her. I tumble over the edge. My cock swells inside her and I feel my balls tighten. "Alice! Fuck! Yes!" She feels so good. I want to hold on to this moment, of watching and feeling Alice Peterson come, and then joining her in ecstasy. My breath comes ragged and heavy as I pull her tighter against me.

We must have fallen asleep this way, because the next thing I know, I'm being awakened by Alice kissing my chest. I'm on my back and she's straddling me, her hair tickling my skin as she traces a line of kisses down my stomach. "This is probably the hottest sight I've ever seen," I tell her. She looks up at me, violet eyes twinkling in the streetlight sneaking through the closed blinds. I've never gone three rounds in one evening before, but Alice makes everything easier.

Afterward, she's like putty, molded against my body, boneless. "I don't think I can go home like this," she says, a hint of worry in her voice.

"You're not going anywhere, Alice," I assure her, pulling my arms around her. "We're going to sleep now, and after I wake up beside you, I want to have you again in the shower."

"Mm I like the sound of that," she says, her voice soft as she drifts to sleep.

Some hours later, we wake tangled together in my bed and the sun shines across Alice's golden, wild hair. I pepper her with kisses and carry her into the bathroom, turning on the shower.

When I redid my apartment, I installed an infinity shower with no door. I typically use the seat in the corner as a shelf for a cold beer after a punishing run, but today I get up close and personal kneeling on the subway tile as I lick every inch of Alice, perched on her throne in my bathroom. She tastes like a ripe peach, swollen and slick with wanting. As she cries out in pleasure again and again, I almost cum without even being touched. We stay in the shower until the water turns cold, and then I envelope her in one of my Turkish bath sheets. The thin cotton towel is big enough for us both, and I like the feel of being cocooned against her.

"This has been the best date, Tim," she says. And she sighs. "But I really have to get home." She kisses my cheek, and rubs the thick scruff that's grown to mountain-man lengths since I last shaved. "Next time, I want to shave you before…" She blushes and looks down.

I notice the red, irritated skin at the tops of her thighs. "Oh shit, Alice! God, I'm so sorry."

"It was worth it, Tim," she says. "I like how you look with some scruff. I've just got really sensitive skin. You should see me after I work with habaneros!" Alice talks to me about her tricks for avoiding contact with hot peppers as I hand her a spare toothbrush from the closet and help her find a pair of shorts that won't fall down.

"Those look like pants on you," I joke. "Unfortunately I don't have any shoes that will come close to fitting…"

Alice stuffs her purse, dress, and shoes into a grocery bag and pulls my arm, walking barefoot to the elevator. I offer to carry her so she doesn't cut her foot, and again when we pull up in front of her house, but she declines. "What am I going to cut my foot on, Tim?"

I don't have an answer right away, but I can't shake my worry that she'll get tetanus or something.

Her brother is out front again tossing a ball around with Alice's nephews. He gives me the stinkeye when I get out to open Alice's door, but she doesn't seem to notice. She kisses me softly and says, "I'll see you tomorrow."

I stand and watch as her nephews crash into her for a hug,

asking where she's been. She looks so happy here, surrounded by this family. They're all tied up in each other's business, but I can see how much love lives in this house. My apartment, sterile and white, feels very empty in comparison once I get home.

CHAPTER TWENTY-ONE
Alice

The next few weeks fly by in a haze. I spend every weekend with Tim, either screwing like rabbits at his house or else eating family dinners at mine. As he dropped me off one morning, my nephews insisted he join us for breakfast. I was surprised that he did, sinking into the couch afterward with my dad and brothers, watching the baseball game on television.

At work, I keep worrying that everyone will be able to tell there's more going on between us, but as per usual, the pace is so hectic we are barely in the same room as one another. I'm pretty sure Juniper caught him kiss me one day when he stopped in for an afternoon snack, but she hasn't said anything.

I'm finishing an inventory order in my office, looking over the schedule for the next week, when my desk phone rings. "Alice Peterson," I say, not looking at the caller ID.

"What are you wearing?" It's Tim. I blush.

"Well, I'm at work, so I'm wearing my chef whites and clogs," I say. "What's up?"

"I've got a big request for you. I'm scheduling an all-day meeting with the Cavs' players union and I'd like to keep them happily well-fed."

"The Cavs? Like from Cleveland? Do we get people from far away like that?"

He laughs. "Well, I certainly hope so, Alice. Stag Law is building quite a reputation. Can you have something together for

Monday?"

"Monday?? Tim, it's Friday afternoon. I wish you'd given me more notice!" I start to panic, looking at the clock and wondering how I'll manage to place orders in time.

"Stay at my place this weekend. I'll help you work on it." His voice is smooth, but it doesn't quite sound like a question.

I sigh. "How many people will there be?" We review the details and I've barely hung up the phone before I start poring over menu ideas.

I start organizing my ingredients lists by the different markets I'll have to visit on the weekend. Most likely, I *will* stay with Tim this weekend, just to have easy access to the vendors in the produce terminal. I'm finishing my notes on a pesto for tortellini--*must make a trip to the Italian market for fresh pasta*--when my cell rings. "Shit. Amy, what time is it?"

"Alice, it's 7 at night! Where the hell are you?" My sister is hopping mad. I was supposed to watch the boys for her tonight so she could go on a date.

"Oh god, Amy, I am so sorry. I'm still at work." I sweep everything into my bag and start running toward the elevator. "Is Dan home? When do you need to leave?" It'll be a half hour or more until I can get home. I remember that I took the bus today. "Shit, Amy, I don't have my car at work."

"Dan was supposed to go out tonight, he says." I can hear my brother complaining in the background.

"Ok, but he's home? Tell him to chill out for an hour and I'll be there as soon as I can." I start to jam the elevator buttons. Of course, today it's taking forever. Of course, our office is on the top floor of huge skyscraper.

"What's wrong, Alice?" Tim slips up behind me. I didn't even realize he would still be here. I turn around and quickly blurt out the whole scenario. The elevator finally arrives and I sprint inside, but he calmly follows and pulls out his phone. "I'll have my driver take us to your house," he says. "I'll hang out with your nephews while you pack for your weekend at my apartment." He grins, still not flustered.

"You're going to come with me to babysit my nephews?" I

raise an eyebrow at him. He's such a renaissance man. Negotiating contracts with professional sports executives one minute and chasing preschoolers around the next. He nods.

"The town car is downstairs waiting for us." He leans in to kiss me, and I forget about the stress of the last few hours, forget that he's the source of the stress. "Tell me what you're working on," he whispers. "I love to hear you talk about food."

He starts to kiss my neck and I lean against the elevator wall. "Well," I say. "Mmm, that feels good. I'm going to make scones for the morning. Lemon...of course...Tim!" He bites my neck and presses me against the elevator wall.

The door slides open and he stands back, straightening his collar. I'm too flustered to walk, and he grabs my hand. "You were saying...lemon donuts?" He opens the door to the Town Car and I climb inside.

"You think donuts?"

He nods. "I don't think this is the tea and scones crowd, babe."

By the time we pull up to my house, we've tweaked the menu into something masculine enough for Tim's standards--basically various cubes of meat served at regular intervals throughout the day. My brother pulls the door open as we hit the porch and he storms out. "At least one of us is getting some. I was supposed to be at the bar an hour ago, Al, and you waltz in here late because you're out messing around with your damn boyfriend?"

"Dan, I was working late and lost track of time and--"

He scoffs at me and shakes his head. "Sure. Working. Save it, Alice."

"What the hell is that supposed to mean, Dan?" But he's already in his car peeling out down the street. My nephews walk out onto the porch as I stand there, shaken up.

"Aunt Alice, what's a boyfriend?" Elijah hands me a jar of bubbles, and I open it, squatting beside him to help him with the wand.

"Well, it's..." I'm not sure what to say.

Tim squats down next to us. "It's me, buddy. I'm your Aunt Alice's friend, and I'm a boy, but I also like to kiss her." He ruffles my nephew's hair.

"My mom says you're Aunt Alice's boss at work, though. Can you have a boyfriend at work?" Eli's eyes are big, and he pauses to blow a series of bubbles into the humid July evening.

"Well, I guess you're not really supposed to," Tim says. "But your Aunt Alice is just so awesome, I really wasn't happy until I was her boss *and* her boyfriend."

This seems to make sense to Eli, who scampers inside, but my brother's angry insinuation has left me uneasy. This is the main problem with my involvement with Tim Stag. He's my boss. Will anyone ever believe my achievements are earned? Tim leans in to kiss the top of my head, then helps me to my feet.

I head off to my room to change and pack for the weekend. When I come back to the living room, my heart melts to see Tim engrossed in a game of Jenga on our dining room table. My nephews egg him on as he slowly wiggles out a precarious brick and the three of them high-five when he successfully places it on top of the stack. I lean against the banister, just watching. He folds into my family so seamlessly. *Maybe I should look for another job,* I think, but I know I'll never find a position that gives me the same creative freedom and independence as this one. This is my dream job, and I know I'll never give it up without a fight.

My phone alarm sounds, my reminder to take my birth control pill. I walk to the kitchen for a glass of water and kiss each of my men as I pass. I won't give any of them up without a fight, either.

CHAPTER TWENTY-TWO
Tim

Having Alice with me the entire weekend has been like a dream, a movie about someone else's happy life. I feel like I'm an entirely different person when I can fall asleep beside her, then wake up wanting her just as badly. She has no background in law, but listened to me when I talked about our strategy for wooing the Cavs to sign with us.

Bringing on a big client from Cleveland will mean travel and long hours, but our firm feels ready for growth. Alice is part of that. I know we haven't known each other long, but something just clicks with her. I might have met someone I can really trust.

Sunday night Alice tells me she's going to make the donuts at my apartment so they're ready for the early meeting. I try to manage my discomfort at the huge mess she's made of the kitchen. "Just stay in the bedroom," she tells me as she weighs flour on a scale on my formerly-pristine table.

I'm pretty sure I don't own half the gadgets she keeps pulling out, and frankly I'm fascinated by this process. "I didn't know donuts were something you could just make at home," I say, wringing my hands so I don't reach for the eggshells she's left on the counter.

"Tim, you know I'm going to clean this when I'm done. You know this. You're making me nervous." She's got a streak of flour on her nose. She's baking in one of my t-shirts and, from the looks of things, nothing else. Even with the AC cranked, the kitchen is scorching with the oil heating on the stove. I catch a glimpse of Alice's ass as she turns to grab a set of tongs, and I suddenly care less about the mess.

"How much longer will this take?" I step behind her, not wanting to get in her way, but making sure she can feel my intentions.

Alice is a stone cold pro, though, and barely responds. "Half hour. Then clean up. Go on, scoot."

I don't want to miss my chance to see her ass again, so I pull up the presentation outline and read it at the counter while she finishes. The second I see her turn off the stove, brushing her hair back from her forehead, I tackle her to the kitchen floor. "I love the way you sound when you squeak," I say, reaching up under the t-shirt.

"I do not squeak," she says, indignantly. "Mm, that feels good. But I thought you wanted me to clean up this mess?"

"I found something I want even more," I tell her. "We'll clean it up together in a few minutes."

In the morning, Alice doesn't look well. Her eyes have dark circles underneath and she moves sluggishly as she gets ready. "Hey," I say, rubbing her shoulders. "What's wrong, sweetheart?" She shakes her head, tells me she didn't sleep well. I chalk it up to nerves and overexertion. "Take tomorrow off, babe. Comp day."

She doesn't respond, though, slowly walking through the motions of packing everything up.

We get ready together, and I think about how easily she fits into my routine. She showers while I shave. We dance around each other to access the mirror and brush our teeth. It feels like *home* with her instead of just a place to live. When we're ready to go, Alice has boxed up the food and tries to balance it with her duffel bag from the weekend. "Babe," I tell her, "don't take that huge bag to work. Come on, we'll get it at the end of the day, ok?"

She nods and lets it drop. She really doesn't look great, but I've never seen her game face before. I figure she might just be focused. We don't talk much in the town car on the way to work, and I peck her cheek after depositing the cardboard boxes for her in the kitchen.

Right on time, the suits from the Cavs enter the lobby of Stag Law, and I hear Donna greet them. I straighten my tie in the mirror. This is it. Time to win a new client, and Tim Stag doesn't lose.

Donna opens the door and I walk confidently toward the six men. "Stag," they say pumping my hand. "Nice place you got here."

"We do our best, Steve. If you could just follow Donna to the conference room we can get started."

Alice must have come in advance to set everything up. She's brought several types of donuts and coffee, procured a fruit tray, and made little dishes of yogurt with granola. Juniper Jones and another of my associates rise to greet our guests. I turn the floor over to Juniper, and I can already tell we've got them eating from our hands. Literally.

Juniper spends the next two hours guiding the conversation. She has read up on this franchise, knows the ins and outs of the players union, and is absolutely flawless describing our strengths representing professional athletes across different sports.

Steve glances over to me at one point, reading some documents, and I jump in, saying, "We represent our athletes through all legal aspects of their careers, from endorsement contracts to workers comp litigation...and we've got a fantastic record when it comes to exploring the morality clause in their contracts."

He laughs and throws the papers back on the table. "In other words, you can make the hookers and blow disappear when you need to." I shrug. *We are in,* I think, but I can't let that show.

The door opens and Alice comes in with lunch. Perfect timing. She sets out the salad and fresh pasta. I can smell the basil and lemon--always lemon with her food--from across the room. I meet her eyes with a smile, but my face quickly falls. Alice looks ashen. She reaches for a pitcher of cucumber water from the cart, and I see her falter.

"Alice," I rise, walking around the table. She looks at me, and as if in slow motion I see her start to fall. "Alice!" Her eyes roll up in her head and she pitches forward. Her temple catches the corner of the table. I reach her as she hits the ground, a stream of blood flowing from her forehead.

"Stag? What's going on here?" The room is on their feet, everyone crowding around Alice.

I develop tunnel vision. I pull her onto my lap. She's still unconscious. "Juniper, call 911," I bark out. Alice groans in pain and brings her hand to her temple. I pull the pocket square from my suit jacket and press it against her cut. I'm not sure if she needs stitches. There's so much blood.

I feel someone's hand on my shoulder, but I won't let go of Alice. I need to know if she's all right. The paramedics arrive and peel me from Alice. Juniper puts her hand on my shoulder again. I hear her this time. "Tim," she's saying. "Tim, she just fainted."

I nod. She's going to be fine. "Because this happened at work, they're going to take Alice to Mercy hospital to get checked out." Juniper keeps talking and I realize we are still in the conference room. The Cavs are still here, retainer contract unsigned. "Would you like me to go to the hospital with Alice or would you like to go?" Juniper pauses. She meets my eye, and I know she knows Alice is more than an employee to me. "Maybe you should go to deal with the paperwork? As her boss?" I nod, and don't look back as I sprint down the hall after the paramedics.

CHAPTER TWENTY-THREE
Alice

My head is pounding. I'm going to be sick. I roll onto my side and dry heave--I haven't been able to eat anything all day. I didn't want to tell Tim I felt sick to my stomach. Today was too important. *Oh shit, what have I done?* I remember going into the conference room with lunch, thinking I could go lie down in my office if I could just make it through this one task.

I didn't really think I had a stomach bug. What happened? As I take stock of my surroundings, I realize I'm on a gurney. I open my eyes and see Tim's face, deeply concerned. "What's going on?" I croak.

He kisses my hand. "We're in an ambulance, babe. You fainted. You've got a nasty cut." I hear the siren, realize the jolting feeling is the ambulance rocking as it hurries down the cobbled side streets behind Stag Law.

"Your meeting," I whisper. "I ruined your meeting."

"No, baby. You didn't. Your health is the most important thing. Juniper's got those guys eating from her hand right now."

The paramedic clears her throat. "Ma'am," she says, coming into my eye line. "We're going to take you in for some imaging when we arrive. We need to know if there's any risk you might be pregnant."

I shake my head. "I'm on the pill," I say, putting my hand to the source of the stinging pain on my forehead. I feel a bandage. The paramedic must still be talking. She's looking at me, expectantly. "I'm sorry. Could you repeat the question?"

"I asked whether you're using your contraception as prescribed. Nevermind. We're going to draw some blood from your IV and do a test."

IV? I glance over to Tim, who looks even more deeply concerned. The paramedic explains they've been giving me IV fluids because I showed signs of dehydration. She pulls a vial from one of the shelves in the ambulance and fills it with blood from my IV access.

We arrive at the hospital and are rushed back to a room, where a nurse helps me onto the bed. A crew of people flock around, asking me questions, shining lights in my eyes. They determine that the cut on my head can be closed with glue, and I close my eyes while everyone works around me. I'm just so tired.

"Are you the father?" I hear a voice as I drift back to awareness.

"Excuse me?" Tim sounds upset.

"The father." I open my eyes. A smiling young woman in a lab coat stands at the foot of my bed with a chart. "Of Mrs. Peterson's baby! I'm the resident, Dr. Shaw. My notes tell me she's expecting!" Before I can register what she's saying, she walks toward me. She continues, "Normally we'd like to do a CT scan to rule out concussion, but it's not really advised for the first trimester. Do you know how many weeks you are, Mrs. Peterson?"

I feel like I've been pushed into a dark tunnel. "It's miss," I say, stunned.

"Excuse me?"

"Miss. Miss Peterson. I'm not married. Did you say pregnant? I don't understand."

She looks puzzled, glances over at Tim, then back to me. Tim looks as though someone has slapped him across the face. "Well, *Miss* Peterson, your blood test came back positive. Did you not know you were pregnant?"

"There must be some mistake," I say, shaking my head until the room starts spinning. "I'm on the pill."

Dr. Shaw looks at her notes. "I see you're taking a low dose pill. Those are very sensitive to timing—you have to take it at exactly the same time every d—"

"I know how the fucking pills work," I spit at her. I'm trying to make sense of what's going on but everything seems impossible. "I have an alarm on my phone every evening." I cover my eyes with my hands. This can't be happening.

"Alarm? Fuck!!" Tim pounds on the bed rail with his fist. "Can you give us a minute, Doctor?" Tim's voice quivers. I open my eyes to see Dr. Shaw backing out of the room. Tim grabs my hand. "Alice...the first night you stayed over...you were asleep..."

Tim confesses that he shut off my alarm, thinking my covert secret phrase was about my nephews. That was what it took. One night. I mean sure. We had sex like 4 times that day I missed my pill...Now I'm pregnant? Pregnant by a man I've only known two months.

I groan. "I think I'm going to be sick again," I say and lunge for the pink basin on the table. Tim steps back as I dry heave into the bowl.

"Alice...what do you want to do?"

I pause in my retching to look at him. "I can't really think about that right now, Tim." I flop back against the bed, hoping Dr. Shaw comes back. "Tim, can you call my sister for me? She works in this hospital."

"We need to make some decisions here, Alice. Decisions...shit." He rakes his hands through his hair, cursing and muttering under his breath. "How could I be so stupid?"

I scoff and then sigh. "I'm not going to terminate anything if that's what you're talking about, Tim."

He holds my gaze for a long time. Then he reaches out and strokes my chin. "We're going to have a baby then." His eyes are wide with wonder, and he gazes at me like I'm some foreign creature.

Tim has the nurse page Dr. Shaw and asks them to find my sister, who comes sprinting into my room a few minutes later. Dr. Shaw has come and gone. I'm diagnosed with a bruised head and morning sickness, with instructions to start prenatal care

ASAP.

Privacy laws mustn't hold for hospital staff because my sister knows everything when she skids into my room. "Alice what the hell?? Pregnant??" She grabs my hands and looks over to Tim, who is now collapsed in the wooden chair like a deflated scarecrow. "Timber fucking Stag, you knocked up my sister!" Amy helps me out of bed and hands me my bag. "I'm going to send you the number for the midwives. Carol has been there so long she caught us AND my boys."

When Tim sees that we are leaving he scrambles to his feet. Amy keeps talking. "You have to wait to tell Dad until I'm there to watch. Oh. And Ryan. Please wait for Sunday dinner and just blurt it out in front of everyone."

"Aim, I'm so glad my crisis is so amusing to you." She steers us toward the exit as Tim calls for his driver to come pick us up.

My sister pulls us both in for a hug. "It's not a crisis! It's a baby!" She claps her hands. "You're both adults and you have homes and decent jobs. This is going to be amazing. I promise." I wish I could share her confidence. Or even make sense of what I'm feeling right now. I huddle against Tim as we wait for the town car. He's wooden and unyielding, gritting his teeth like he can chew right through this challenge.

When Joe pulls up, I don't even wait for anyone to open the door. I collapse into the back seat and close my eyes until we start moving.

"Wait, where are we going?" Joe is headed west along the Allegheny River, not east toward my house.

Tim looks at me, utterly perplexed. "I'm taking you home. To rest. So we can talk."

"Tim, I want to go to my house, to sleep in my bed and to think."

Tim shakes his head. "Alice, we need to talk this through. This is ...you're not thinking clearly and... Alice! A baby. *Our* baby..."

My head is pounding. I can't think. "Joe, please take me to my house." Tim starts to protest, but I cut him off. "I just really need to be alone right now, Tim."

When we finally pull up to my house, I'm surprised to see both my brothers are home, but then I remember it's late afternoon and we've been at the hospital since lunchtime. When Tim opens the door and I climb out, my brothers leap from the porch and come running to me.

"What the fuck, Alice? Who hurt you?" My brother Ryan balls his hands into fists, glaring daggers at Tim. "Stag, if you so much as laid a finger on her, I swear to Christ I will end you right now."

"Relax, Ry. I just fell at work." Tim's mouth opens, but no sound comes out. I glare at him. "Tim drove me to the hospital and I'm fine. No stitches even. I'll probably have a black eye, though." I'm babbling again. My brothers don't seem quite appeased, but I'm so exhausted and I'm feeling another wave of nausea. "Look, guys, I just want to go to bed. Tim, I'll see you on Wednesday."

"Alice, wait."

"No. I really just need to go to bed." I start to walk into the house.

He moves to follow, but Dan puts his hands on Tim's chest. "She said she's good, dude."

"Alice, I'll bring your things over later. Please call me when you've slept." He looks desperate, and part of me wants to go to him, but if I stay upright another second I'm going to puke and cry all at once. I close the door, hurry up the stairs, and collapse into   my   bed.

CHAPTER TWENTY-FOUR
Tim

Pregnant.

Alice is pregnant.

I got my girlfriend pregnant, and we haven't even had a conversation yet about whether she *is* my girlfriend.

All through my teens, I expected this to happen to my brothers, probably Thatcher. Part of me waited for this type of phone call in college. And now I'm the idiot who fucked a girl with no protection. And what the hell was I thinking, shutting off her phone alarm and not telling her? I never let myself assume anything...so much for following my own advice.

I don't even recognize who I've become.

Shit. The meeting.

"Joe, can you take me back to the office?"

He looks at me in the mirror. "Are you sure, Mr. Stag? You're not looking so hot."

"Joe. Office. Now." I don't have time for people's assessments. I need to get hold of Juniper Jones.

"Right away, sir." We head west, Joe avoiding the highways and finding a back road to avoid the rush hour traffic. I pull out my cell and breathe a sigh of relief that I've got Juniper's number. Donna must have programmed it in for me.

I punch the screen to call her up and, almost like she was waiting for my call, she answers after one ring. "Tim."

"Juniper. Give me some good news."

"Tim, how is Alice?"

Shit. Of course she's concerned about Alice. Everyone probably is. Alice knows everyone, knows their food preferences and knows the names of their damn grandmas. I breathe deeply. "Just a cut and a shiner. She'll be back on Wednesday."

"Everyone will be so relieved," Juniper says. She covers the phone and shouts this news. "We all have been hanging out waiting to hear an update. I tried calling Mercy, but of course they wouldn't release anything. I even told them I was her attorney, but I was very relieved they insisted on protecting Alice's health information--"

"Juniper! The Cavs! What happened??"

"Oh! Oh, Tim. It was fine. You know they were so impressed with everything this morning. They took the contract with them to review, which is customary, but I'm certain they'll come back with a yes and a retainer check tomorrow."

I exhale the stress of the past few weeks, the part of my mind that focuses on work feeling much needed relief. Juniper continues. "Should we give some thought as to who will service this account? It will mean a lot of travel to Cleveland and our scan of the news lately seems to indicate we'll have our work cut out for us with the hookers and blow, as Steve so delicately put it."

It never occurred to me that anyone other than myself would handle this client. I delegate the less prestigious work, but this has been the prize I've been eyeing ever since I got my brother Ty back and signed. "Juniper, I really appreciate how you handled that meeting today. You were poised and professional and, really, quite excellent--"

She cuts me off. "Tim, if I can be blunt, I'm not interested in taking on this client. The travel would take away from my training time."

Shit. She thought I was buttering her up to give *her* the Cavs. "Of course, Juniper. I plan to work this client personally. I was just making sure to praise your work in getting them here."

"Oh." There's silence on the other end. "Well, thank you, Tim. While I have you, I really want to discuss the ideas I mentioned for the firm."

"Juniper, I'll be at the office in ten."

"You're coming back today?"

"Yes. What do you mean?"

"Well, I just thought...don't you want to stay with Alice?"

"I'm not interested in pursuing this line of conversation right now, Juniper. I'll see you in ten minutes." I hang up on her. Things have never been this complicated for me. Just keep my nose down, work on the plan, account for all potential complications. Even with our dad drifting in and out of the house, I managed to keep our financials together, keep my brother Ty in private school for hockey. I scoff at the memory of forging my father's signature each month to deposit our mother's life insurance payments while he drank away his sorrows in one dive bar or another. At least they had their ducks in a line before she passed so we didn't lose the house.

And here I am about to have a child, unable to even get my shit together at work let alone my personal life. This shouldn't feel so complicated. Haven't I already provided for my family? Haven't I already made sure my brothers found success? Even if my middle brother defined that differently from the rest of us. I shake my head, twist my fisted hands in my eyes to clear the cobwebs. I need to sit at my desk where I can think.

Juniper meets me at the door and we walk and talk. I'm only half paying attention to her ideas. I'm sure they're good ones, and I actually trust her to pursue them, so I don't file that as urgent. Instead, my mind drifts to the Cavs contract and what I need to do to make sure Alice and the baby are safe, protected, and cared for. I settle into my chair and start to work out the logistics   of   my   plan.

CHAPTER TWENTY-FIVE
Alice

I wake up to my sister rubbing my leg. "Al, babe, let's talk."

I sit up and collapse against her chest. Her strong hands rub my back and she mutters soothing words into my hair. I'm the only one of the Peterson kids to inherit my mother's curls. Unruly and wild, just like Dad always says she was. "Hey," a thought occurs to me. "Do you think the baby will have curly hair?"

Amy laughs and I burst into tears again. It starts sinking in that a real human is growing inside my body right now. A baby our mother will never meet. "Amy, what am I going to do with a baby?"

She laughs. "What do any of us do with babies? You'll do the same thing you did with my babies. He or she will hang out and watch baseball with Dad and the uncles. But shouldn't you also be talking about this with Tim?"

"Oh God, Amy, I am so overwhelmed. I love where things had been going with him. But now everything is going to change. And Tim hates kids. You should have seen how he reacted when the kids were at the office."

"Alice," Amy's hand is firm on my shoulder. "I've seen him with the boys. He's great with kids. It sounds like he just doesn't like surprises. Remember how I told you not to just take the boys to work with you?" She flips on the light and reaches into the pocket of her scrubs.

"Here." She says, handing me a card. "This is the number for the midwives. This is the same practice Mom saw for each of her pregnancies. I wouldn't imagine going anywhere else."

I exhale. This is too much reality for a Monday. "Hey, Aim?"

"What's up, Al?"

"I just want to go to sleep for now, ok?" She kisses my forehead and slips out, turning off the light. I sink into the mattress and sleep until mid-morning.

It's strange being in the house alone during the day. There's no commotion, no noise. Everyone is at work or school. I'm alone with my thoughts and that appointment card for the midwives...and a phone that seems a little too silent. I guess I was expecting Tim to call by now. I make myself a cup of coffee, wonder if I'm allowed to have coffee, and decide to call and ask before I do anything else.

The nurse schedules me for an intake appointment and answers all ten thousand of my questions. I'm relieved to learn there's really nothing in my life that needs to change apart from cutting out craft beer and turning off the now-useless alarm reminding me to take my birth control pills. They email me some information and a recommended book list and I decide to spend the day reading it all and shopping at the bookstore. All in all, I'm feeling much better despite the nasty bruise. With some careful adjustment of my curls and a scarf tied around my hair, I'm able to hide most of that when I head to the bookstore.

I return home an hour later to see Tim sitting on my porch with his head in his hands. He looks...not good. His hair stands on end and he's wearing the same suit as yesterday. "Jesus, Tim, are those spots of my blood from when I fell?" His shirt is stained. I've never seen him look like this.

"Alice! Where the hell have you been? I've called you 100 times."

I look at my phone and notice that it's still set to Do Not Disturb from when I went to sleep last night. "Oh, Tim. I'm sorry. I had it--"

"Let's go, Alice, we need to get your things."

"What are you talking ab--"

He grabs my hand and snatches the keys from me, unlocking the front door. "You need to pack your things. I'll have someone come to get them and move them for you."

"Tim, what the hell?" He looks stunned. "Have you even slept? Tim, I'm concerned about you right now."

He shakes his head. "No, Alice, I haven't, but it's fine. I figured it all out."

He launches into some convoluted explanation that evidently involves me quitting my job, moving into his apartment and--"Wait. Tim, did you just say marriage?"

"Of course." He looks at me like I've got spinach in my teeth. "We have to get married. My child will be a Stag."

"Tim, we don't need to get married for the baby to have your last name. But this is besides the point. Everything you're saying is just...it's too much right now."

"Alice, if you think for one minute that I'm going to live separately from my child and his mother, you are gravely mistaken."

I shake my head. "Tim, just wait."

He looks manic. "I've made some calls. You'll be seeing the best obstetrician in the tri-state area and we'll schedule your delivery the day after the due date. Everything will be safe and controlled, Alice. Especially once you stop working. You can focus on the baby and staying healthy!"

I blink my eyes, not wanting this to be really happening. "Timber Stag, if you think for one minute I'm moving into that sterile wasteland you call a home you are out of your damn mind. And quit my job? Really? To be what? Barefoot and pregnant at your house? What makes you think I even want to be with you if this is how you really feel about raising babies?!"

I didn't really mean to say that, because of course I want to be with Tim. But Tim as he's been the past few weeks. Not this maniacal, safety-obsessed madman with bloodshot eyes. How is he going to respond to late night wakeups if just knowing about the baby has him insisting I quit my job?

My words have cut him. I can tell. "Look, Tim, we both need to cool down and think here."

"You don't want to be with me?" His voice wavers and I can tell this is not something he had considered as part of his "master plan." "But it's my baby, too...it's my baby, Alice. I have to keep the baby safe."

"Tim, you've had a shock and you're exhausted. You need to shower and sleep. I'd like you to leave now and go do those things. We can talk tomorrow." He lunges for me, and I duck past him into the house. I have no idea how he's going to respond right now. "You should call Joe to drive you," I shout through the open window. "You shouldn't drive like this."

"ALICE!" he pounds on the front door. "Let me in right now." I close the window and sit on the couch, clutching my shopping bag to my chest. This is just not how I ever imagined starting a family. This isn't what happened when my sister got pregnant. I screw my eyes shut tight. *She was married and had been with Doug for three years* I remind myself. Tim persists. "Alice! You cannot do this. It's my baby, too, God damn it!"

When I open my eyes, my Dad and brother are standing in the kitchen. They must have come in the back door together. "Alice, pumpkin, want to tell me what's going on before I call the cops on   this   guy?"

CHAPTER TWENTY-SIX

Tim

After Alice's brothers chased me off their property and threatened me with a PFA, I wandered the park until dark. And then I couldn't figure out what to do next, so I sat down next to the fountain to watch fireflies. I have no idea what time it is. My phone is in my car, double parked where I screeched to a halt outside the Peterson house.

I hear someone approaching, but don't look up. The massive forms of my brothers come into my line of vision, and I grunt by way of greeting when they sink down into the grass next to me. "Been looking for you, bro," Thatcher says. "Gran is beside herself. You were supposed to take her to dinner today."

Shit. What day is it? "Is today Tuesday?" I look from one brother to the other. "How did you find me?"

Ty slaps a hand on my leg. "Listen, Timber. Juniper told me what happened during the Cavs meeting, and then she told me you holed yourself up in your office covered in blood, and then she told me you tore out of there muttering to yourself about some plan of action."

"Why the hell is Juniper calling you with that information?"

Ty lets out a long breath. "She's my lawyer and she's worried about you and she knows I'm your brother, dude. And we all know you've been fucking Alice Peterson. And I know your car is parked half-assed in front of her driveway because I went over there to move it for them." I close my eyes, but Ty keeps talking. "AND we know her family thinks you're a fucking lunatic.

Thatch, does that cover everything?"

Thatcher grabs hold of my other leg. "Almost, baby bro. I believe the Petersons said something about a shotgun, owing to the fact that our brother Timber seems to have gotten Alice Peterson pregnant."

"Right." Ty starts talking again. "So. Talk to us, bro, and then we're taking you home to get cleaned up."

Thatcher hands me a bottle of water, and I suck it down gratefully. And then I tell them all of it, starting with my inability to stay away from Alice since the first second I saw her. I tell them how she has consumed my thoughts, how good it felt to have her at my apartment. How terrified I've felt since the minute the doctor said she was pregnant and I realized it was my fault.

Thatcher puts his arm around my shoulder. "Tim," he says. "You've been on watch for a long time, man."

"On watch?"

"Yeah. On watch. Watching out for us, day and night, around the clock. Since mom died. But from what I've seen and from what you're saying, it sounds like Alice helps you let your guard down." I nod. "It's ok to let your guard down, Tim-bo. You know that, right? You don't have to be the one in control all the time..."

And then we sit in silence for awhile until they help me to my feet. Ty climbs into the driver seat of my car and I start to protest, but they push me into the back seat. I fall asleep and don't wake up until we pull into the garage in my building. My brothers walk me into my apartment. It really is a sterile, empty shell, just like Alice said. Thatcher procures a six-pack and my brothers camp out on my couch while I shower. I don't even like being in my fancy shower without Alice. Nothing feels right. I'm worried I fucked everything up with her and she won't ever come back.

I walk to the living room after I shower. Ty hands me a beer and looks at his watch. "We keeping you from something, Tyrion?" Thatcher doesn't let anything slip by.

Ty shrugs and looks around my apartment. "This place sucks,

Tim."

I frown. "What do you mean by that?"

"Do you even live here? There's, like, nothing here. Just furniture."

"I've got pictures of you clowns," I say, pointing to the wall across from us. But he's right. That's the only personal touch in the whole place. I really don't spend much time here, and once I took Alice's bag to her house, all the little things she had set around this weekend were gone, too. I take a long swig of my beer. "I fucked up, guys."

Thatcher doesn't look away from the TV. "We know, bro."

We sit in silence for awhile and eventually I fall asleep. I wake up to the sun streaming in the windows.

Alone.

CHAPTER TWENTY-SEVEN
Alice

After I finish hurling up my breakfast, I take a deep breath and head into work. I try to arrive before everyone, but there's a stream of well-wishers coming into the kitchen. Everyone has heard what happened by now and wants to check on me. I know they care, but it makes me feel a little like a freakshow as they ask about my black eye. The bruise from my forehead has sunk down so my whole cheek is purple and green. There's no hiding it.

So far, Juniper has helped me spread the story that I was so focused about catering the Cavs meeting that I didn't eat or drink anything. It was a really hot day Monday. Nobody has trouble believing I passed out from dehydration. I make sure to keep a huge glass of lemon water nearby at all times. Lemon is about the only thing I can consistently keep down. Whatever else this baby is, he or she most certainly is not interested in food. *Definitely doesn't take after me,* I think.

Once the first big wave of Stag Law employees heads back to their offices, Juniper hangs around in the kitchen. She bites her lip and looks at me. "Want to go get some coffee and talk?" she asks. "I thought about calling you yesterday, but wanted to give you some space."

I exhale deeply and nod. It will feel good to talk to Juniper. We head toward the elevator together. There's a coffee shop across the street, and I try ordering mint tea. Juniper and I grab a table near the back and as soon as we sit, she says, "Look, I know there's something more going on with you and Tim. And I want to be someone you can trust to talk about that." I open my mouth to speak and she holds up a hand. "I want to prove that you can trust me, because I need a friend to talk to about something, too. So I'm just going to tell you--I'm sleeping with Ty."

My jaw drops. "Ty *Stag?*"

She nods and takes a long sip of her drink. "It started before I even knew him. I needed to move on from...well, I needed to get laid, and I picked him up in a club. I had no idea who he was. You should have seen my face when Tim said he wanted me to represent his brother, and his brother ended up being that nameless guy I fucked in a bar bathroom."

"A bathroom? You? Jeeze, Juniper. This is all...well I'm really surprised."

She raises an eyebrow at me. "You know more than anyone how irresistible the Brothers Stag can be, right?" We share a laugh. "So tell me what's going on. Maybe I can help? Or just be a friend at least. I'm new to this city, and there aren't enough women at work."

She's right about that, which I remember she had planned to speak with Tim about last time I talked to her. "I slept with Tim during one of Ty's hockey games," I tell her and brave a sip of the mint tea. My stomach seems to accept it gratefully.

"Oh my god, Alice! The first playoff game where the whole office came to watch! I remember you snuck off for a 'tour' of the arena!" She laughs. "So this has been going on for awhile."

I tell her how at first we were just infatuated, how we both thought we could get it out of our system. "But then, I don't know. It just started to feel like more. He really opens up to me, and I really like how that feels."

Apparently things are going the same for Juniper and Ty. It sounds like her feelings for him are stronger than she's even admitting. For a brief minute, I let myself fantasize about us being sisters. Then a wave of nausea washes over me and I cram a crumpled napkin against my mouth.

She starts pushing a drink stirrer around in her empty cup, then says, "So look, Alice, I care about you and I care about Tim. He's a good boss and a good guy. I just want you to know that you can talk to me. Because it sure seems like the other day was about more than a bumped head and dehydration."

I bite my lower lip and nod, not trusting myself to talk without crying. I haven't actually said the words myself yet. Even the nurse on the phone at the midwifery practice had access to my medical records from the emergency room when my sister made the referral. But if Juniper is in a relationship with Ty, she's going to find out soon. I'm sure Tim talked to his brothers about what's going on. Or at least I hope that he did. Juniper looks at me expectantly, and I figure everyone is going to know soon enough, anyway. At least I'll have an ally when I have to run off and hurl while I'm serving lunch. My voice is barely above a whisper, and I tell her, "I'm pregnant."

Juniper breaks into a wide smile. "Alice! That's so exciting! I mean, I guess it must be a shock for you. But I was afraid you had cancer or something. Seriously, this is the best news!" And then she's run around the table to hug me. To my surprise, I let her, and it feels really good to have a friend like her around. I tell her a little bit about Tim's breakdown. She doesn't seem surprised, telling me how he wouldn't come out of his office until he stormed out of the building. She apparently called Ty and he came to get Tim's car from outside of my house.

By the time we walk back up to the office I'm feeling ready to forgive Tim for freaking out--he'd had a shock, after all. Now seems as good a time to go talk to him as any, and Donna gives me a warm smile as I approach the executive office. "Is he in, Donna?"

"He is! Do you want me to buzz him for you? He's just reading over some contracts that arrived this morning from Cleveland."

"No, Donna, that's ok. I'm just going to go in and...thank him...for helping me on Monday." She nods and returns to her computer screen as I push open the door.

Tim's desk is covered with papers, and he's turned to face out the window. He stares out at the river below, looking peaceful and contemplative. I gently clear my throat and he spins around to face me. "Alice," he says, his voice quiet and questioning.

"Can   we   talk?"

CHAPTER TWENTY-EIGHT

Tim

Alice offers me an opportunity to explain my behavior, which, given the way I yelled at her and pounded on her door, seems like more than I maybe deserve right away. "I'm so frightened, Alice."

She walks around the desk and reaches for me. I rise to hug her, and as soon as I have my arms around her, I feel so much better. She's solid and real and as I hold her, I begin to think that maybe this can eventually be ok. "I'm here, Tim," she whispers. "I'm scared, too." She starts to cry softly against my chest and I stroke her hair.

We hold each other like this for awhile until Alice says, "I know we have a lot to talk about, but I'd like it if you came with me for my first prenatal appointment later today."

"Of course! Alice, I want to be at every appointment. You need to understand that this is my top priority. You are my top priority. That's why I panicked the other day."

She squeezes my hand. "Tim, I know you panicked. But you have to know that there aren't going to be one-sided decisions here. You're not, like, the king who hands out the laws for me to obey."

"I know that, Alice. I know. God, I'm such a fool." I pound my fist against the desk, stirring the papers. I turn to the window again, looking out at the river. "I don't know what the hell to do, Alice."

"Do you have to decide today? Can you *talk* to me, Tim? What are you thinking about right now?"

I gesture to my desk. "This...Cleveland...the Cavs. I've been chasing this client for almost a year, Alice. A year. This is a signed retainer contract and right now I don't feel like I can accept it." She sits and I explain how I don't want the travel anymore. I don't want to spend half the week heading to Cleveland and miss ultrasounds or birthing classes. I want to assemble the crib and just be present. "Alice, I want to be all in for this."

"Tim, neither of us has to give up our dreams because I'm pregnant. You know it's not just the two of us, right? Like, you understand that my family is going to be very, very involved in this baby's life? That's not negotiable for me. And I'd really like Baby Stag to have some Uncle Stags around, too."

Fuck me. Uncle Stag. I hadn't even thought about my family's response. I try to imagine Thatcher holding a baby and realize I can't even picture *myself* holding a baby. Alice stands up. "One day at a time, ok? Just meet me in the lobby at 2 to head over to my appointment." She walks out of my office and I can tell this round of Deep Discussion is over.

After lunch, where I try not to bother Alice in her element, I call for Joe. I realize I'm not sure where we are heading exactly, so I tell him to hold tight on our destination. She stands by the elevator waiting. I don't even stop to think about it, but I walk right up and kiss her on the cheek. She blushes and looks around to see if anyone is watching. "I don't care who sees, Alice. Things are different now."

We ride down to the lobby in companionable silence and Joe is parked right out front with the town car. "Where to, Miss Peterson?" She smiles at him and fires off an address I don't recognize.

A short ride later, Joe pulls up beside some nondescript building near an industrial complex. There's murals of women painted all over the outside. Alice climbs out of the car and walks toward the door. I follow, skeptical. "Alice, what the hell is this? Did you cancel the appointment I made with the obstetrician?"

She turns to face me. "Tim. First of all, you never graced me with the name of this fancy obstetrician you keep talking about. And second, I told you. No unilateral decisions. I'd like you to come and meet the midwives who worked with my mother and sister."

I follow her up the stairs, past the wall of photographs of babies and their half-naked mothers. *Midwives?* "Tim!" she shouts at me and I catch up to where she's signing in at the registration desk. This isn't going well.

The receptionist smiles at me. "Congratulations, Dad! We've got paperwork for you, too. Just your basic family history stuff." She slides me a clipboard. I start sweating. Alice plunks down on an armchair. This place looks like someone's living room. I walk over to her. "Alice, I really would prefer a *medical* provider."

She doesn't look up at me. She starts scratching away at her forms until a woman comes out the doorway. She has gray hair tied back in a loose ponytail. "Welcome to the Midwife Center, Alice!" *First names?* She's not even wearing scrubs. I really want to drag Alice out of here, but she grabs my arm and pulls me over. "And this must be Timber. Right?"

I grit my teeth, but return her handshake. "Tim."

I try my best to hold an open mind while she chats with Alice about being present for her birth. Ok, so it's obvious this woman has been around awhile. She catches me staring at her and says, "We get a lot of nervous dads here, Tim. What questions can I answer for you today?" I shake my head and stare away toward the wall. "Let me see if I can guess." She puts the clipboard on the desk and stands, rummages through a filing cabinet and sits back down on the padded chair. "You're thinking we're a bunch of witches with cauldrons cackling over herbs and smoke. Am I getting close?"

I scoff at her. "Your words, not mine."

She laughs. "You hate that this isn't some sterile examining room and you're thinking your baby would be better off under the care of a skilled surgeon. Am I there yet?" I shrug. She throws me a pamphlet. *Midwifery 101: A Guide for Nervous Partners*

"Is this a joke?"

She turns serious. "No, Mr. Stag. Prenatal care is serious work. For the record, I, and many of my colleagues, received advanced training from Yale and the University of Pennsylvania. I've caught over 4,000 babies, including your partner. I'm happy to discuss the advantages of midwifery care for healthy women with normal pregnancies. You clearly have reservations about our facility, and I'm offering you an opportunity to discuss them before we begin Alice's examination."

I'm taken aback by her tone, overwhelmed by all of this. I'm not sure what possesses me, but before I've made a conscious decision, I stand and storm out of the office. I stomp down the stairs toward the street, trying not to notice the photographs along the wall.

Until I see it.

Near the middle of the staircase, beaming in a black and white photograph, is my mother. She holds a tiny child, face contorted in its first wail. My mother. My mother was a patient here, too.

CHAPTER TWENTY-NINE
Alice

I try not to cry after Tim storms out of the midwife's office. She pulls me into a hug and asks me to talk about how I'm feeling. She has such a warm personality and I love knowing that she's hugged my mother with these same arms. That she knew me as an infant. I might not be able to ask my own mom any questions about pregnancy, but it helps knowing I can ask this woman who cared for my mom during that time. I tell her how this pregnancy was unplanned, that my relationship with Tim is still new and we are clearly on rocky ground.

"Unplanned does not mean unwanted, Alice. I want to make sure you know that." Carol makes some notes in her file. She reviews some of the information with me about the do's and don'ts of a healthy pregnancy and hands me a prescription for some bloodwork. We talk about my cycle and she estimates I'm about six weeks pregnant. We make a plan for my next few visits and then she gets ready to give me a tour of the center.

They've got a number of nature-themed birthing rooms with regular beds, rocking chairs, and whirlpool baths. Carol even shows me the nitrous oxide I can use if I feel like I need pain management. She takes my arm. "Would you like to see the room where you were born?"

Would I? "I'd love that!" I tell her, and she walks me to the staircase. I'm stunned to see Tim standing there, staring at the wall.

"Mr. Stag?" Carol says, her voice kind and calm. "May we help you with anything?"

He points to a picture of a woman and baby. She's radiant, glowing, smiling down at her precious child. "This is my mother," he says. "Laurel."

Carol smiles and drapes an arm over his shoulder. "It appears your family shares Miss Peterson's history with our practice," she says. "Laurel Stag was one of our first patients here nearly 30 years ago. We were about to show Alice the Desert Room where she was born. Would you like to join us?"

"She's beautiful, Tim," I say to him. "Look how happy she was to be a mother." I reach for his hand, and am glad he accepts mine in his. We walk around the birthing room, with its soft colors and peaceful decorations. Carol shows us how the dresser drawers contain medical equipment for various situations that are unlikely to come up.

"Most likely, your midwife will need little more than a pair of rubber gloves, if your birth goes anything like your mother's or your sister's!" Carol smiles warmly and says we can take all the time we need to explore before we head out. She heads off to greet her next client and leaves me with Tim and all of our baggage.

"Want to sit," I ask him, gesturing toward the upholstered bench in one corner. I lean my head on his shoulder, still feeling the thrill and spark when our skin connects. I have feelings for him. I want to be with him. But I can't let him call all the shots like he's been trying to do.

"I messed up, Alice," he says.

"I know," is my reply. "Want to tell me what you're thinking about?"

He takes a deep breath, and tells me about Sunday pancakes with his grandmother. "She's been adding cinnamon lately, ever since she talked with you about it," he says. And he talks about going running with his brothers, nearly keeping up with Ty even though he's a professional athlete and Tim and Thatcher are just your average fitness fanatics.

"I like hearing about your family, Tim. I'd like to spend more time getting to know them."

He nods. We sit together a while longer, and he asks--his voice apprehensive--"Did I ruin everything, Alice?"

"No, Tim! It's all just...heavy. You know?" I lean in to softly kiss his cheek, relishing the smell of him close by. "Let's just take things slowly, ok? We have 8 months before anything needs to change."

He wraps his arms around me and I can feel him relax as I let him hold me. "What comes next?" His voice is soft, his fingers in my hair. He feels safe and warm and his vulnerability right now, the way he's trusting me to see this soft side of him--I realize this is what I want more than anything else. Just to be open and raw and real with him and to hold each other.

"How about you take me out to buy some prenatal vitamins and   we'll   go   from   there."

CHAPTER THIRTY
Tim

The next few weeks are probably more stressful than prepping for the bar exam after only 2 years of law school. Every day, I have to drum up the courage to tell Alice what I'm afraid *might* happen and talk with her about how we both think we should respond to everything from breastfeeding to circumcision.

I never imagined I'd enjoy reading about the female reproductive system, but I'm finding all the pregnancy information to be fascinating. Alice and I look at those "pregnancy week by week" websites and she bases each week's menu around whatever food they've said our baby is supposed to be that week. Of course she does. Once it got out at work that we are together, Alice has told anyone who will listen how excited she is to have a nursery here at Stag Law. Alice and Juniper have a plan to make this the most family-friendly workspace in Pittsburgh.

I do like that she's making plans, but I still feel strongly that financial planning is crucial. I've got Alice on board to start a college fund immediately and we've got life insurance policies in place for each of us, but she isn't ready to get married yet and refuses to move into my penthouse with me. I feel like it's reasonable to live five miles from her family, but she says if our child can't walk over to visit Grandpa, we live too far away. And, she insists, my place is too barren. I've offered to paint and remodel, but she says we need to agree to disagree that the penthouse is an acceptable home.

At least I got her to agree that we should all live together. I can't bear the thought of sleeping apart from her and it kills me to do so now. She's so tired after work that I usually drive her to her family's house and she goes right to bed. The pamphlets say this is normal for the first trimester, that she's working so hard growing a brain and organs for our child that she's exhausted.

I don't have to hold myself back from kissing her when I see her, but I have to say, after a month, I'm wild with desire for her. I can see her body changing subtly and she looks sexier than ever to me. I want to tell every single person I see that this woman is growing *my* child inside of her. And then I want to ravage her.

I glance up at the clock. I've got about a half hour before we need to leave for Alice's next midwife appointment. We're going to try to hear the heartbeat today and I'm so eager for that sound, it feels like the seconds are scraping by. I take a last look at the papers on my desk, comb over everything one final time, and hand the stack to Donna to have them delivered. "Donna, I'll be out the rest of the afternoon. Would you be able to overnight these? I trust you implicitly."

"It took you long enough, Tim Stag," she says, laughing.

"Truly, Donna, you're excellent at your job. I'm thankful to have you by my side." Donna blushes and I rap the side of her desk with my knuckles as I walk down the hall.

Alice's face lights up when she sees me. She hangs her chef coat on a hook and I admire her as she heads toward me. This beautiful woman is mine. Sort of. She's carrying my baby and I intend to keep working until she's mine officially, legally, and all ways there are to belong to someone. "I made a decision about the Cavs account," I tell her as we wait for the elevator.

"Tell me."

"I declined to take the contract. I don't want to do all that travel and Juniper declined it, too. There isn't anyone else at Stag Law I'd want on that specific client and..." I shrug. "It just didn't seem important to the big picture.

Alice stands on tiptoe to kiss me. Her mouth is soft and warm and I take a minute to just savor how she feels. "I'm glad, Tim."

"If I would have known you'd kiss me like that I would have declined clients earlier." Alice punches my shoulder playfully. I really like how things are between us right now.

The whole way to the Midwife Center we talk about how excited we are to hear the baby's heartbeat, but the truth is I am anxious. I think once I hear that sound, I will feel more comfortable that everything is safe. For now. Alice rushes through Carol's questions, eager to get to the finale. She tucks her shirt up and wriggles her pants down her hips just a little. I try to control my dick when I see the creamy white skin of Alice's still-flat stomach. When Carol asks if I want to direct the Doppler I'm terrified, but Alice smiles at me and I squirt the goo on the wand. I aim where Carol suggests, right below Alice's naval. The room fills with a swirling static sound that pulses until...there it is. The steady, strong beat of my child's heart. The ticking music brings me to tears and I drop the wand, overwhelmed by this proof of life in Alice's body.

Here is this tiny force, a piece of me and of Alice, outside my control yet depending on my protection. "Everything sounds perfect, Alice. Just perfect." Carol helps Alice wipe off and sit up. "Baby's heartbeat is strong!" She makes a note in Alice's chart and tells us to take our time leaving.

I crawl up on the table with her and pull her into my arms. "That was magical," I say, kissing each of her knuckles, splaying my hand across her stomach. She nods. She looks so satisfied, so happy. I want to tell her what I've been thinking about this week, but I'm worried she will think I am being too controlling. I really am trying hard, but I have been taking charge for so long. I am not used to consulting someone. "Could I take you somewhere, Alice? I'd like to show you someplace I think you could be happy raising our baby."

"Tim..."

"I haven't signed anything or done anything. I just had this idea the other day and I'd really like to share it with you if you'd let me."

She nods. I leap down from the table and scoop her into my arms. "I was hoping you'd say yes. I've done so much today I never thought I'd do and all of it just feels so right."

"Put me down, you crazy fool." Alice has laughter behind her voice and once again I'm giddy with anticipation of showing her my idea. I help her into the Volvo and head toward the neighborhood where we grew up. Her eyes question my actions as we drive closer until I finally park in front of my grandmother's house. The house where I grew up. "Tim, what is this?" She asks.

Alice has only been here once or twice since we got together, but it occurred to me the other day that it's a lot of house for one old lady to live in alone. "Hear me out." We walk to the front door and I fish for my keys. "You know Ty finally moved out. I was standing in his empty room the other day and I got an idea."

I guide her up the stairs into Ty's room, which faces south. Two huge windows look out upon the neighborhood. Light streams into the room, with its built in bookshelves and beautiful floors original to the house. "I kept imagining a little boy playing cars there in the square of light from the window. Or a girl reading books on a carpet here."

Her eyes are wide as she stares at me, but she doesn't speak. Not yet.

I pull her down the hall to the next room. "This was my room as a kid." My grandmother has been using it as a guest room, so there are twin beds and a dresser in here, but not much else. "There's room here for a king sized bed and there is *just* space for a crib here in the turret. I know you want the baby to sleep in our room for a while because of breastfeeding." I can't get a read on Alice's face. Now it's my turn to babble. "I mentioned to my grandmother that you wanted to raise the baby close enough to your family that he could walk over for a hug."

I walk to the window and beckon Alice to follow. We lean forward. The leaves are just starting to show signs of changing. "Once the leaves fall, we have a clear view of the Peterson house," I tell her. "But for now you just have to squint a bit and you can see it. Your dad could be waving at us from the window for all I know."

"Tim." Her voice is a whisper. My heart races with

anticipation. I want her to want this, to want me. "This is perfect." And then Alice is kissing me the way I've wanted to be kissing her for weeks. Her tongue parts my lips and I accept her gratefully, moaning as I taste her. She leans back against the window for support and I press my weight into her small body, loving the curves and warmth against my chest. "Is your grandmother home now?" I can feel Alice's apprehension mixed with desire. I hope I'm not misreading her desire.

I shake my head. "She's out playing cards this evening. She'll be gone for hours."

Alice is a woman transformed. She places two hands flat on my chest and shoves me across the room until I land on the small bed. I pull her down onto me and just enjoy making out with her, slowly and hungrily, until I feel like I might burst. "Alice, I've missed this so much," I tell her, shifting our bodies so I'm on top of her, nestled between her legs.

"I love that you want us to live here, Tim," she says. "I love *you*." Her words cause my blood to race.

"I love you, too, baby," I say, breathless with emotion. "I've loved you for so long now. I just didn't know what to do with that before now." She smiles and those violet eyes meet mine. Her hands reach for the tails of my shirt, pulling and fumbling. I quickly unbutton it and toss it across the room while Alice lifts her own shirt over her head. "Holy shit, Alice!" Her breasts are huge, heaving as she breathes in the fading light of sunset. "Can I…" she pulls my hand against her chest, and my fingers knead the soft flesh, thumb circling the hard, hard point of her nipple.

I dip my tongue against the other breast, sucking through the thin material of her bra. She arches her back against me and I reach behind her to pull off this barrier between our naked chests. "God, you feel so good," she says, as her hands explore the skin of my back. I've missed the feel of her soft palms against me, her curious fingers that work such magic with food. As I suck each swollen teat, Alice groans and reaches for my waist. I lift my hips so she can slide down my trousers, kicking them off as they get past my knees.

"Your body has changed so much, Alice, already." I pepper

kisses all along her stomach, circling her naval, feeling the firm fullness of her lower belly. "You're so fucking beautiful." I ease myself down her body, taking her pants and panties with me until I'm kneeling on the floor at the foot of the bed.

I reach for her ass and tug her toward the edge of the bed, draping each beautiful leg over my shoulders. "Oh, Tim! Please!" she moans as I reach between her legs, parting her soft curls and finding her slick with wanting.

I tease her folds with my fingers, one hand massaging her nipples, enjoying the look of pleasure on her face. She bucks her hips against my hand and begs. "Please, Tim. I need you." I spread her pink center and dip my tongue against her, and she begins to moan like I've never heard her. I love that I brought this out in her, that I can take her to this place. Deep, animal groans escape her mouth as I lave her with my tongue. I don't stop until she's screaming, her pussy pulsing around my fingers, practically pulling me inside her body.

"I love to watch you come, Alice." I hold my hand flat against her center until she stills. Easing out of my boxers, I crawl back onto the bed. She parts her legs for me, wraps them around my hips, and I slide inside her with one smooth thrust.

I have never felt more at home. She reaches for my head, pulling me against her mouth, the taste of her on both our tongues. Slowly, I move with her, sheathed fully inside her beautiful body. I adjust my weight so I'm supported on my forearms and Alice runs her hands along my pecs as she lifts her hips to meet mine. She grinds against my pelvis, circling to find the friction she needs to come again.

"I love you, Tim Stag," she says, breathlessly, and then she erupts. She screams my name again and again until I can't hold back anymore. I burst inside her, groaning, feeling our wet heat combining, and we both sink slowly into blissful silence.

"I love you, Alice." I roll to my side, still joined with her, not ready to separate, and hold her close. "I'm never going to let you go."

Epilogue: Tim

8 Months Later

Alice finally agreed to marry me in early May. Our families gathered in her parents' back yard and one of my friends from law school, now a judge in the city courts, officiated. Alice's wild hair hung long and loose, spilling down her back and around the deep green dress that hugged our baby.

The round form of our son jutted from Alice's front, taut and centered so you'd never know she was pregnant from the back. As I pulled her in to kiss her after our vows, I felt him kick and admired his timing.

A few days after the ceremony, Alice carries the final box into our kitchen. She began sleeping here with me as soon as we finished painting and all the fumes dissipated. We sold my penthouse and have been gradually rearranging so the house is ready for Baby Stag. Gran decided she was more comfortable on the third floor, despite all the stairs, and it seems like every corner of our home has fresh life in it. Alice has added plants, family photographs, and soft rugs. Every room has a quiet place to sit, with a stash of baby supplies.

She's really taken this musty old house, full of sadness and grief, and transformed it into a place of love and life and hope. I take the box from her hands--her cookbooks are far too heavy for someone 40 weeks pregnant--and pull her into my arms. "Mrs. Stag, you should be resting."

"Mr. Stag, I feel restless!" she giggles. "I keep having this feeling there's something else I need to be doing, but I can't figure out what it would be." She shrugs and lets me massage her shoulders. "Mmm that feels nice."

I move so I'm standing behind her, pulling her close against me, massaging her shoulders and rubbing her arms while I kiss her neck. I twist her hair around my fist and lift, blowing gently on the nape of her neck. "I can help you find an outlet for that nervous energy," I tell her. When she groans I let my hand drift lower, lower, meeting the heat of her core.

"Tim." Her tone shifts, her body stiffens under my hands.

"What's up, babe?"

"I'm having a contraction."

My hand shoots instinctively to her belly, where I feel the strong muscles tighten and eventually soften. "It's really happening! Ok, what do we do?"

"Now we just walk and wait," Alice says, pulling my hand. She asks me to text her sister, who of course tells her brothers and they somehow reach my brothers. Soon enough, our house is full of aunts and uncles taking turns rubbing Alice's lower back, breathing with her as she walks up and down the stairs.

A few hours later, Alice can no longer talk through her contractions and she tells me it's time to head into the Midwife Center. I freeze, momentarily terrified. I'm not ready. How can anyone ever be ready for this? My brothers squeeze my arms, and I look at them. "You got this, big bro," Thatcher says. "We'll be right behind you in Amy's minivan."

I nod and, breathing slowly through my nose, I help Alice into the back seat of the Volvo. I try to help her with her seatbelt, but Alice shoves my arm out of the way. She isn't talking right now, breathing through pursed lips. She leans backwards over the seat. "You're not going to buckle up? Alice, that's--"

"Tim, just fucking drive." She nestles her head in her hands and I see that there's no getting around this. She groans as I drive through the night, much too fast for neighborhood roads. "Next time I think we should just stay home," she says, in between contractions.

Carol greets us at the door and ushers us quickly inside the Desert Room. As quickly as Alice is able to move, in between groans and long contractions. I ask Carol if she's planning to check Alice's progress, but Carol smiles as Alice moans long and deep. "No need to check anything, Tim. Your wife is about to birth this baby."

The second we cross the threshold, Alice drops to her hands and knees. I move around front of her to meet her eyes. She locks her gaze onto mine and puts her hands on my shoulders. She starts panting and I can see her body squeezing. Her body is pushing a human being to the outside. "Alice, you're so amazing, sweetheart. You humble me right now, baby."

She can't speak. She's not blinking and I don't dare break her gaze until suddenly, she starts breathing easily again. "The head's out," Carol says softly. "Alice, reach down and feel your baby." I'm frozen in awe, looking down to see the dark curls of our son. "One more big push and he'll be here with us." Carol puts a gloved hand on my shoulder. "Tim, why don't you reach down and catch your babe?"

I don't even pause to think that I have no idea what to do. Alice groans one final time and I reach out to lift the slippery, pink, howling child my wife just brought into the world. Sobbing, I hand him to Alice. Because it's a him. A son. I have a son. She gazes down at him, euphoric, kissing him everywhere. Peter Stag is here to change everything. Somewhere in the distance, I hear Carol congratulating us, telling us he's healthy and that Alice is perfectly fine.

Somewhere in the distance, I hear my brothers and Alice's siblings spilling into this room that's no longer a desert but an ocean of love. At the center of it, amid all the cheers, kneels Alice, looking radiant and exhausted. When I meet her eyes again, she is so much more than she was a second ago. My wife, my world, the mother of my son. I lean in to kiss her and wrap my arms around this family that will make me whole and teach me every day to let go and trust. "I love you," I whisper to them both. "I love you."

Curious what comes next for Tim and Alice?
Click here for a steamy bonus scene!
BookHip.com/BKZNLV

Dying to know what comes next for the Stag Brothers?
Ty Stag's story continues in Filled Potential.

Made in the USA
Monee, IL
13 March 2023

29796903R00080